# WHITE KNUCKLE RIDE

Publisher's note: variations in spelling are consistent with the original publications.



First published 2014 by
FREMANTLE PRESS

Fremantle Press Inc. trading as Fremantle Press
PO Box 158, North Fremantle, Western Australia, 6159
fremantlepress.com



Cover design Ally Crimp.
Cover photograph Getty Images, 'Moment Open'.

A catalogue record for this book is available from the National Library of Australia

ISBN 9781925161250 (paperback)

Fremantle Press is supported by the Western Australian State Government through the Department of Cultural Industries, Tourism and Sport.

Fremantle Press respectfully acknowledges the Whadjuk people of the Noongar nation as the Traditional Owners and Custodians of the land where we work in Walyalup.

CRIME FICTION BY

ALAN CARTER x AMANDA CURTIN
PETER DOCKER x JON DOUST
DEBORAH ROBERTSON x DAVE WARNER
... AND MORE

# WHITE KNUCKLE RIDE

FREMANTLE PRESS

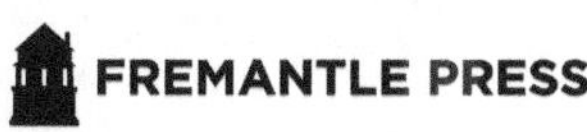

# CONTENTS

# ALAN CARTER
# FISHY BUSINESS

**Wednesday, October 8th, 2008. Late morning.**
**Katanning, Western Australia.**

The way the body was lying, it was obvious she hadn't seen it coming. The limbs were splayed at a grotesque angle. A pool of blood beside the head had dried in the sun before it could make it the few centimetres to the side of the road. Blowflies hovered impatiently. The October sun was high and unseasonably nasty. Anybody with any sense was sitting under the shade of the only tree for miles. Or they were somewhere else.

The sergeant was crouched beside the rapidly ripening corpse, talking into a small digital recorder. Cato Kwong squinted at the sergeant and took a swig of lukewarm water from a bottle that felt like it was melting in his hands. On his iPod, *La Bohème* was reaching a screeching crescendo. He turned it off and removed the earphones. He checked his watch. Time seemed to move so slowly these days. The sergeant's name was Jim Buckley: he chattered to himself, loving every minute, every detail of the task at hand. For a big bloke his movements were graceful. Pavarotti in a butcher's apron.

'Bullet number one entered just behind the left ear and exited through the right cheek; bullet number two entered the left eye. No apparent signs of an exit wound so we presume bullet number two is still lodged inside. I now intend to conduct an on-the-spot autopsy to confirm. Recording suspended at ... 10.22 a.m. Detective Sergeant James Buckley.'

Buckley reached over and opened his toolbox. He pulled out a handsaw.

That's one big difference between Homicide Squad and Stock Squad, Cato mused, you don't have to wait for the autopsy, just do it yourself. He was still getting used to the idea: Detective Senior Constable Philip Kwong—Stock Squad. Homicide Squad, Major Crime, even Gangs, they had a ring to them that made you puff out your chest and stand a bit taller. Stock Squad? They were there to deal with cattle duffers, sheep theft, stolen tractors. They were touted as industry experts, they knew the farmers, knew the lingo. In Cato's view they were washed-up has-beens recycled as detectives. Mutton dressed as lamb? The Laughing Stock Squad. So if you come across a suspicious cow will you take it back to the station and grill it? Or leave it to stew?

So far Cato felt like little more than a glorified agricultural inspector. Stock Squad. It kind of escaped from the corner of your mouth like a coward's curse. Coward's curse pretty well summed up his situation. He was here because he'd been hung out to dry by a bunch of cowards he'd once worshipped and he couldn't do anything about it because of the Code, the Brotherhood, the whatever other bullshit name that might conceal a multitude of sins.

The Stock Squad was on tour: hearts and minds. The other two members of the squad taking the high road to the north, Cato Kwong and Jim Buckley on the low road south. A week of 'intelligence gathering' was how Buckley saw it: pressing the flesh, nosing around, random checks and a healthy per-diem budget—it would keep them in piss until they got back to Perth. A week of chewing straw, swatting flies and nodding sagely at stuff he didn't give a rat's arse about was how Cato saw it.

Cato Kwong: Stock Squad. Cato, like Peter Sellers' Chinese butler and martial arts sparring partner in *The Pink Panther*. A nickname inflicted on him at police academy. Cato hadn't seen any of the movies so he'd rented the videos to see what they were getting at. Cato, the manic manservant? Cato, the loyal punch-bag? Or just simply Cato the Chinaman?

The beginning of day three and Cato felt like he'd been on the road for a month.

'Oi, Kwongie, you gonna give us a hand, mate?'

Jim Buckley was already red-faced with effort as the saw bit into the back of the cow's neck. Blood spurting, blowflies going berko, he was in hog heaven. Cato winced primly; he preferred his meat plastic-wrapped and barcoded.

'Jim. Sir. Sarge ...'

Cato still didn't know how to address Jim Buckley. It wasn't that he didn't have any respect for authority, it was just that he was still working on it in Jim Buckley's case.

'Look, do we really need to do all this stuff? It's pretty obvious. The cow was run over, finished off with a couple of bullets to the head. The back leg was chopped off with a chainsaw and taken home to the barbie. End of story.'

Cato took another swig of the mountain spring water. He didn't function well in excessive heat. Maybe he should join the Canadian Mounties, or the Tasmanian ones, somewhere nice and cool.

Jim Buckley frowned, a tad disappointed with the younger man's attitude. 'It's still a crime, Cato mate. And it's our job to find the bad guys.'

Cato knew he was banging his head against the proverbial. Buckley, after twenty-five years in the force, had finally found his niche. Stock Squad was Jim's domain and he was in no mood for negativity. He mopped a sodden brow with a wipe of his shirtsleeve and passed the blood-soaked implement to Cato.

'So, as your senior officer, I'd advise you to shut the fuck up and start sawing.'

**Four hours earlier. Hopetoun, Western Australia.**
Her lungs were bursting and her left hip was agony: two kilometres from home and four behind her. For the last twenty minutes she'd been feeling a bit old, worn out. Too many twinges these days and getting harder to keep them at bay. But then she rounded the corner, hit the top of the sand dune and there was the ocean. Beautiful, she thought, gorgeous. A slight breeze rippled the surface and the sun was just coming up, dispelling the shadows on the hills in the national park over to the west. The huge open sky was striped orange, pink, purple, and blue.

And would you believe it, dolphins, two of them, splashing in the shallows near the groyne. She semi-sprinted the last two hundred metres along the sand where it was packed hard at the water's edge, never taking her eyes off the dolphins. As she drew nearer something changed. The way those dolphins were moving, the shape of the fins, the frolicking and splashing; no, it wasn't splashing—it was more like thrashing. Sharks. And there was something in the water with them, something brown, floppy, lifeless. A seal maybe, from the colony on the rock a few hundred metres out from the groyne. She quickened her step. This would be something a bit special to share with her primary class in news today.

One of the sharks seemed to be shaking the seal in its jaws, like a puppy with an old sock. Finally it let go and the seal flew a few feet through the air, landing with a soft plop at the water's edge. From five metres away she could see they'd ripped the poor little bugger to shreds; just one flipper remained and the thing didn't seem to have a head. She was right on top of the carcass now. She stopped, caught her breath, shivered. It wasn't a seal; it was a human torso. It wasn't a flipper; it was an arm—a left arm, no hand. She'd been right about the head though—there wasn't one.

She bowed forward, hands on knees, and threw up. Behind her she could hear the sharks still splashing in the shallows like a couple of dolphins, playfully taking the piss.

Hot flush. Senior Sergeant Tess Maguire put down her coffee, opened her jacket and cracked a car window. The smell of rotting roadkill nearby forced her to shut it again, quickly. Tess swore and flicked on the air conditioning. Six-twenty on a sharp, spring south-coast morning and she was sweating like a pig. Suddenly cold again, she flicked the air conditioner back off. She felt completely out of sorts. How could she be getting hot flushes when she'd only just turned forty-two? Tess looked at herself in the rear-view. The short-cropped blonde hair was losing its fight against the wispy greys. She kept on threatening to let it grow out to all-over grey. It was natural. What's so bad about grey anyway? She tried to think of some attractive, well-known, grey-haired women. She couldn't get beyond Germaine Greer. Tess added hair dye to her mental shopping list and turned the radio on.

The interviewer sounded young enough to be her daughter. She'd countried her voice up a bit, talking with an authoritative twang to a primary commodities broker about the grain and wool prices. Apparently one was up and the other was down, in contrast to the stock market in general which was still in freefall. Tess couldn't get her head around how a handful of venal mortgage-brokers in America could trigger what seemed to be a global financial tsunami and the end of the world as we know it. Never mind, it was unlikely to hit them here in Hopetoun—the end of the world and proud of it. This was Tess's first posting since she came off sick leave. Nine months. Most of the first month in hospital and outpatients, the next three in physio, the rest in therapy. She wondered how Melissa would go: new to town, year nine in high school, sharing a classroom with a bunch of teenage hard-cases whose dads had come down to work at the new mine. She'd seen them hanging around the park—the kids, not the dads. Testosterone. The pushing and shoving, swearing and shouting: youthful high spirits, some called it. Only these days it sent her into cold sweats and panic attacks, fighting for breath, tears welling up. Even now, just at the thought of them.

A new life, a new start, new hope in Hopetoun, they'd promised her. The place hadn't warranted a permanent police post in the past. For decades it had been a laid-back holiday or retirement spot for wheatbelt farmers. There was nothing to police except maybe the occasional drunk driver or domestic. Now, with the nearby nickel mine, the population had steadily grown from a stable four hundred in the old days to a whopping two thousand—and rising. It would still be a while before it was Gotham City, but with more houses, plenty of money being tossed around and the pub getting busier it meant more bad behaviour, temptation, vandalism, domestics and drugs. Hopetoun was a good place to put ageing or wounded or useless cops out to pasture. Tess ticked all three boxes. At first she'd turned it down. Senior Sergeant Tess Maguire—the bump up to 'Senior' was a reward for getting the shit kicked out of her—wanted to tough it out. But after a few weeks at a desk in Perth HQ with the concerned but embarrassed stares, the traffic, the noise and the crowds, Tess was sold on the sea change. Hopetoun. No crime to speak of, she reasoned, no stress, just sunshine and sea breezes to clear out the cobwebs.

As the sky brightened, Tess passed a convoy of white utes heading in the opposite direction out to the mine, forty kilometres away. On the outskirts of town she climbed the low hill to the roundabout leading off to the light industrial on one side and the new sprawling off-the-peg Legoland housing estate on the other. Cresting the rise she relaxed a notch or two at the view down the main street to the bright blue Southern Ocean at the bottom of the hill. After three months she still hadn't got over how small, quiet and, yes, beautiful the place was. And she hoped she never would.

Tess pulled into the beachside gravel car park. Her colleague, Constable Greg Fisher, was on the beach talking to a middle-aged woman dressed in running gear, while the town GP crouched examining something on the sand; it was hidden from view by a makeshift canvas windbreak. Greg's initiative: he was in his first year out of police academy and eager to impress. Tess had long forgotten that feeling. A pair of pied oystercatchers pecked the sand irritably with scarlet stiletto beaks. A small handful of early-rising onlookers strained to get a glimpse of the body, careful not to overstep the invisible line established by Constable Fisher.

As she got closer, Tess recognised the woman as a teacher from the primary school: she'd seen her around, hard not to in a town this small. The teacher was a bit green around the gills; her eyes were puffy, her lower lip trembled as she talked, Greg taking notes. Tess left them to it and walked, white sand squeaking beneath her feet, over to the doctor and the body. The torso glistened in the morning sun; green tendrils of seaweed sparkled on the mottled, lightly tanned flesh. There was no head, no legs, only part of one arm and a pale grey mush where the missing pieces should have been.

The doctor stood up, broad-shouldered, early fifties. Tess had met him once before, a few weeks back when she dropped in a young miner who'd been on a bender and tried to punch out the pub ATM when it argued with him about his PIN number.

'What's the word, Doctor Terhorst?'

'Well he's dead, that's for sure.' His lip curled slightly at his little joke, then he continued in his clipped Afrikaans accent. 'But at this stage I can't accurately say what age bracket or even, for sure, what race. From the torso length I'd estimate medium height, medium build. Don't ask me for a time of death, with something that's been in the water it's too hard without the proper tests. Ball park? Less than a week.'

'Shark attack?' Hopetoun. Southern Ocean. Not an unreasonable question.

'Well I've seen a few of these back in Cape Town and the injuries are consistent with sharks.'

Tess pointed to the mush at the base of the spine where the legs were meant to start. 'Looks like they bit clean through him.'

The doctor nodded grimly then scratched his chin. 'Possibly. I'd be more worried about the sever wound at the neck.'

'Why?'

'It's very neat compared to the punctures and tears everywhere else. The spinal column looks like it's been sheared with a clean straight edge. Either our shark had meticulous table manners ... or somebody cut this poor man's head off.'

Sergeant Jim Buckley was heaving, puffing and fit to have a coronary. His normally flushed drinker's face was nearly purple and his ginger-grey sideburns glistened with sweat. The cow's head was now separated from the body after a joint effort by himself, Cato and three hacksaw blades. Its neck was flat to the ground and the eyes were staring skywards to cow heaven. Buckley had a foot planted firmly on either side of the head, pinning the ears to the ground. With his left hand pushing down hard on the nose for extra leverage, he gave one last mighty tug with the right. His hand emerged triumphant from the cow's face, pliers gripping a small blood-soaked lump of metal.

'A .22, just as I thought.'

Cato finished pissing against a ghost gum and zipped back up. He had retired to the shade and was halfway through today's cryptic from the *West*. He'd managed to snaffle it from the neighbouring breakfast table at the Katanning Motel. It had been a close shave though, the guy had only gone to the toilet and when he came back for his paper Cato had to plead ignorance and suggest that the breakfast lady had cleared it away. Buckley had shaken his head in disgust.

'Why don't you ever buy your own, they're only a dollar, you tight-arsed bastard.'

'Dollar thirty. All I need is the crossword, I don't need to read all the other crap.'

His father had taught him how to crack the cryptic codes a couple of years ago and now he was hooked. There was something about the search for clear reasoning among the insane ramblings, and identifying the cold calculation behind the crafty wordplay. It came in useful in the interview room sometimes. Dad meanwhile had moved on to Sudoku to enrich his widowed dotage; he'd knock them off in ten minutes if his hands weren't shaking too much. He'd tried to get Cato onto it, reckoned the process of patient, logical elimination would be good for training his detective brain. Cato was sticking with the cryptics; intuition, flights of fancy, twisted logic and inspiration backed up later by the facts—that was more his style.

*Merit Cup for perfect roast.*

Cup, roast, something to do with coffee? The heat was curdling his brain. Cato stretched out his long legs and smiled encouragingly.

'Good work, Sarge. Any idea whose gun it came from?'

Jim Buckley's good mood had withered in the heat.

'Get fucked. Bag this evidence while I clean up.'

'What, the head as well?'

'In the esky; sooner it's on ice the better.'

'No worries,' Cato sighed. He wondered if he should resign now or after next payday. That was the intention after all: disgraced, demoted, demeaned, despised—until he had taken enough and went of his own accord. They wouldn't sack him; he knew too much. But they certainly had their ways.

Cato grabbed a Ziploc bag out of the Land Cruiser glove box, hauled the esky off the back seat, and kick-closed the car door, planting his heel dead centre of the bull's-head logo. He popped the bullet in the bag and crammed the head into the esky. A mobile buzzed in his trousers. It took Cato by surprise; he hadn't expected a signal out here.

'That you, Cato?'

'Detective Senior Constable Kwong speaking, who's this?'

'Hutchens.'

DI Mick Hutchens, his old boss from Fremantle Detectives. Now with Albany Detectives, enjoying a south-coast sea change in Bogan Town. He'd fared better in the fallout than Cato had.

'What can I do for you, sir?'

'Cut the crap, it's me, Mick. Where are you?'

Cato looked around at the parched, blistered landscape.

'Somewhere near Katanning.'

Hutchens chuckled. 'Enjoying life with the Sheep-Shagging Squad then?'

'Not sure the Commissioner would appreciate your cynical tone, sir.'

'Right. That fuckwit Buckley with you?'

'Want a word with him?'

'No. Listen up. Got some real work for you. A body, well, half a one anyway. Human though; would make a nice change for you.'

Cato's pulse quickened like it hadn't done for a long time.

'Where is it?'

'Down in Hopetoun; maybe three hours drive for you.'

Cato racked his brain—Hopetoun, south coast, fishing spot? Other than that, the place meant nothing to him.

'Why aren't your mob onto it? I'm supposed to be banished to Siberia, remember?'

A momentary uncomfortable silence, then Hutchens cleared his throat.

'Three are on suspension, two on sick leave, two on holiday. I'm scraping the bottom of the barrel. Thought of you immediately.'

'Cheers.'

The faintest whining hint of desperation crept into Hutchens' voice. 'Cato mate, I need you. For the next few days anyway.'

Cato couldn't shake the thought that there was more to this than met the eye. Was Hutchens really scraping the very bottom of the barrel before he thought of his old mate Cato? The sun scorched the back of his neck, flies worried his face, and the headless three-legged cow was starting to smell really bad. The road out of Katanning shimmered in the heat haze. Who was Cato Kwong to look a gift horse in the mouth?

'Tell me more.'

'Washed up this morning. Looks like a shark attack but the local doctor reckons our bloke might have been dead before he hit the water. He's a country quack so probably talking through his arse.' Same old Mick Hutchens, thought Cato, Zen master of the sweeping generalisation. 'I need you to take a look, confirm or deny. No hassle, no fuss. Fill out the paperwork and file it, Cato. Home by Friday.'

Cato had lost track of time—then he remembered, today was Wednesday. If it really was that simple and clean-cut he'd still be home in time for the weekend. It was his turn to have Jake. They could have a family weekend together, just the two of them. Yeah right.

'Who's the officer-in-charge down there?'

'Senior Sergeant Tess Maguire ...' Hutchens paused, no doubt for effect. Cato didn't miss a beat, didn't give Hutchens the reaction he wanted.

'Taser Tess?'

'The very same.'

After her ordeal at the hands of the mob up north, the Commissioner had made taser stun guns standard issue for all officers in the optimistic belief that the outcome might have been different had she been 'suitably equipped' with a fifty-thousand-volt zapper. Cato had his doubts about their effectiveness in that kind of situation, particularly if they fell into the wrong hands. Scepticism aside, it had made Tess something of a folk hero among her colleagues right around the state. She had been more than that to him, once.

'I thought she'd left the job.'

'Sent to Hopetoun. Same thing. Look, take Buckley with you to make up the numbers but mate ... keep him away from those sheep.'

Hutchens signed off with a 'baaaaaah'. Cato sighed and snapped his phone shut. Then it came to him, *Merit Cup for perfect roast.*

*Merit Cup*: an anagram, 'Prime Cut'. It was enough to turn a good man vegetarian.

Jim Buckley was hunched over by the wing mirror, mouth pursed, using a Kleenex baby wipe to try to get the bloodstains off his Stock Squad shirt. Cato coughed politely for attention.

'Sarge. Something just came up.'

They should have been in Hopetoun by early afternoon but Jim Buckley had insisted on backtracking to put the cow's head into storage in the freezer at the Katanning cop shop. The local boys weren't happy. They'd have to find somewhere else to store the snags and steaks meant for this Friday's sundowner barbie.

'Use some initiative,' Buckley had snapped at them, rather ungratefully.

Then they'd stopped along the way for a late lunch: two meat pies, a Mars Bar and a Coke for Buckley; for Cato just the one pie, a floury bruised apple and an orange juice, having caught sight of himself in a window and seen what just half a week on the road can do. Then there were the four smokos and two piss stops. Then they'd pulled up a couple of speeders and issued tickets, Buckley getting his stats up, Cato getting his blood pressure up. He was impatient to get to the body. He wondered if Buckley ever felt the thrill of stuff like this—a possible case, a mystery: was the body dead before it went into the water? That kind of thing. Probably not. He caught a glimpse of himself in the rear-view mirror—flecks of grey at the temples but, at two months short of thirty-eight, he was in as good a shape as he had been for years. The banishment to Stock Squad left him with extra time on his hands and he used some of it to get fitter. Swimming, cycling, and avoiding the kind of junk he'd eaten when he was doing normal cop hours—whatever they were.

Recently Cato didn't seem to be able to get enough sleep. There was a time when he buzzed along on four or five hours. Nowadays he usually got the full eight, often more, but still sometimes woke up exhausted and lethargic. Today? Today he saw a flicker of energy in his eyes that he hadn't seen for a long time.

It was midafternoon by the time they crested the rise that would drop them down into Hopetoun. The suffocating heat of the interior had eased as they neared the coast. The hot easterly had become a fresh south-westerly and Cato was beginning to feel halfway human again. As they rolled down the Hopetoun main drag—Veal Street it was called—Cato reflected they were having a big meat-themed day. Cows' heads, gift horses, barbies, pies, even the crossword solution. And now Veal Street; that's life in the Stock Squad.

Two telephone boxes stood outside a cafe where a handful of people drank coffee on a pine deck. In one of the booths was a man with his back to them, wearing dusty blue and fluoro-yellow work overalls and holding one hand over his free ear trying to block out the wind noise. He turned to face them and Cato saw that he was Chinese. Their eyes met for a moment as Cato rolled past.

'More than just the one of you in town then,' Buckley observed.

Cato continued looking at the man through his rear-vision mirror.

'Well spotted. That must be why you're the sergeant and I'm a mere constable.'

'*Senior* constable: don't put yourself down, mate,' Buckley corrected him.

Cato had phoned ahead and got through to Hopetoun second-in-command, Constable Greg Fisher. Greg told him to meet them at the Sea Rescue hut beside the skate park. He had forewarned them: the hut was the cop shop until the new whiz-bang multipurpose emergency services building was finished. It might take a while, he'd said, 'chronic labour shortage'. From what Cato could see—a big pile of sand inside a temporary wire fence—there was little evidence the new cop shop had even been started. He pulled up onto the rust-coloured gravel. The Sea Rescue hut was a faded and peeling olive-green and about the size of a shipping container—but not quite as pleasing to the eye. The door was open so Cato walked in. Greg Fisher was sitting at a desk talking on the phone. He looked up and acknowledged the visitors with a wink. Senior Sergeant Tess Maguire stood by a recently cleaned whiteboard, the smell of cleaning fluid hung in the air. She had a red marker pen in her left hand and Cato noticed her bare ring finger. In the centre of the whiteboard she'd given the body a name, 'Flipper', and drawn a question mark beside it. Over to the right-hand side, a short list of names and telephone numbers.

She turned. At first glance she still looked the same Tess to Cato but, on closer inspection, her eyes seemed darker and sadder. She was using them to measure him up too. Cato sucked his stomach in a little bit and lifted his head to give his neck more of a chance but Tess seemed to be more focused on the bull's-head logo on his Stock Squad breast pocket. Cato winced inside; he really needed to change back into civvies at the first opportunity.

'Nice uniform; heard you were coming to town.' The light seemed to have gone out of her voice as well. 'How's things?' she inquired idly, like the answer didn't matter.

'Good. Good.' He said it twice as if to reassure himself.

Cato introduced Buckley who was, after all, the senior officer. Tess filled them in on what little she knew: teacher, sharks, torso, doctor, head (lack of).

'Why Flipper?' Cato nodded towards the whiteboard.

Greg Fisher failed to smother a grin. 'The teacher who found him thought it was a seal at first, thought the arm was a flipper.'

'Do you get many people dropping in here?'

Cato could see Tess bristling.

'There'll be a room divider up by tomorrow,' she said. 'No member of the public will see the board.'

Cato wondered how you could divide such a small space any further. Callous nicknames aside, as the days went by there would be plenty of other reasons why the information board would need to be blocked from public view.

'So tell me about the doctor's take on this.'

Jim Buckley clearly thought it was about time he asserted his presence. 'Yeah, has he been watching a bit too much telly, or what?'

Tess summed up what she'd been told, finishing with the news that the body had been carted up to Ravensthorpe, fifty kilometres away, and put into cold storage in the hospital there.

Cato swore. They'd had to come through Ravensthorpe to get to Hopetoun; he could have checked out the body on his way through—if somebody had bothered to let him know. Now they'd have to waste time backtracking. Greg looked uncomfortable. Cato could see that Tess didn't give a hoot: this was her patch, her rules.

'A pathologist is coming over from Albany; he should be at Ravensthorpe in a few hours. You can meet him there. Anything else you want to do while you're waiting?'

She had addressed the question to Buckley, letting Cato know who was boss. Buckley looked over at Cato. Detective Kwong took his sunnies out of his Stock Squad shirt pocket.

'Let's go to the beach.'

The beach at Hopey didn't offer any major new insights but Cato enjoyed the squeak of the brilliant white grains under his Stock Squad blundies and the sparkling clarity of the water rolling and crashing onto the shore. For him it was as much about getting a feel for the place, the lie of the land and all that. First impressions? Small. The tour of the town had taken about five minutes; there seemed to be about half a dozen streets either side of the main drag. East of Veal Street were mainly older holiday shacks; to the west, the newly built Legoland—as Tess called it—courtesy of the mine. At the south end of Veal Street, the town centre—three shops, a couple of cafes, a park, a pub, the beach, the ocean. At the north end, Veal Street became the Hopetoun–Ravensthorpe Road. Hopetoun was the original one-horse town and, at first glance, a beautiful and peaceful place to die.

Cato had asked Tess and Greg to find out tide and weather conditions for the last few days to see if that would tell them where the body might have entered the water. He also suggested following up any missing person reports from the last few weeks or so. Tess had given him a 'No shit, Sherlock?' look. Obviously, in both instances, she was already on the case. Cato should have expected the hostility from her but it still bothered him.

It was at least twelve or thirteen years ago but it was clearly a sore that had never properly healed. And why should it? Cato was fairly fresh out of the academy and four years her junior. They had been partnered up, working nights out of Midland, Perth's bandit country, in the souped-up unmarked Commodore. Cato Kwong—Prince of the Mean Streets. High-speed chases through the suburbs, domestics, prowlers, break-ins. Routine stuff but still usually more a thrill than not in those days. And the adrenaline had fed the spark between them. It all seemed natural and inevitable and it was good, great at times. All over each other like a rash. Until he walked out on her.

It was nearly dark as they drove into Ravensthorpe. Just a few pale strips of sky lay in the west, sandwiched between the silhouette of distant hills and a blanket of ink-black clouds. Ravy, as it was known locally, was bigger than Hopey, only just. The main street was dark and deserted except around the two-storey red brick Ravensthorpe Hotel where an array of utes and four-wheel drives were angle-parked in anticipation of the Wednesday night pool competition. Some of the utes bore mine company logos. Cato had seen the lights of the mine off in the eastern distance as they passed the airport turn-off halfway between the two towns. You couldn't miss it, a patch of brilliant daylight in the surrounding dim dusk. They'd had to pull into the side of the road while an ambulance, with lights flashing, sped past.

Cato pulled into the hospital car park and killed the radio. According to the eight o'clock news the Australian stock market just had its worst day in twenty years. Jim Buckley snorted and muttered something to the effect of 'Boo-fucking-hoo'. It was deadly quiet, not many lights on. Like many country hospitals, Ravensthorpe was little more than a glorified nursing post, kept open by the skin of its teeth, the marginality of the electorate or, as in this case, the persuasive power of the mining company. The ambulance, having deposited its patient, was swinging back out onto the road; the driver and Cato exchanged a relaxed hand-flick wave.

Cato and Buckley approached the front entrance expecting the automatic doors to slide open. They didn't. Except for emergencies, the hospital operating hours had recently been cut back to an eight to eight shift. 'Staff Shortages' said the handwritten notice blu-tacked to the door. It was 8.05. Cato rang the bell and they waited. And waited. Cato cupped his hands to the door and peered through the glare for any signs of life or movement inside. Nothing. He swore loudly and pressed the bell a tenth time. Finally an elderly woman in a pink dressing gown floated into view with a cup of something steaming. She almost dropped her mug as she saw Cato's face up against the glass. He pressed his ID against the door mouthing 'POLICE'. It didn't help; in fact she seemed even more determined to hurry back to her bed and hide under the covers.

Jim Buckley stepped forward with a kindly smile, a cheery wave, and a non-Asian face. That seemed to do the trick. The old woman poked a button on the inside and the doors slid open. With a bedside manner that was a complete revelation to Cato, Buckley got directions to the operating theatre at the rear of the hospital as well as learning all he needed to know about her hernia and cataracts.

'Thanks Deirdre, and you take care of yourself now, love.'

'Are you coming back tomorrow, Roger?'

'Yes love, 'course I am.'

Buckley gave her a last little wave and led Cato down the corridor. Cato wondered who was meant to be looking after Deirdre overnight when he spotted a grumpy-looking woman with angry red hair knotted up in a bun. She was coming out of the ladies. She didn't give either of the men a second glance, as if strangers wandering the hospital corridors at this hour was an everyday occurrence. Instead she thumped through a set of double doors behind which Cato could hear muffled cries and commotion. Dear Diary, remind me to avoid needing an overnight stay in Ravensthorpe General and to never whinge about city hospitals ever again.

The lights were at least on in the operating theatre, a good sign. They pushed open the doors and walked through. A short wiry man paused, scalpel in hand. Behind him an assistant sat on a stool at a steel bench in the corner taking notes with one hand and eating a sandwich with the other. She didn't pause or look up from behind her curtain of black hair. In the other corner stood Tess. She looked at her watch meaningfully and smiled mock-sweetly.

'So you found the place okay.'

Cato's patience was stretched paper-thin. 'Had a bit of trouble getting in.'

The man with the scalpel was obviously keen to get on with it. 'Evening gentlemen, you must be the detectives. I'm the pathologist. Harold Lewis, Harry to you. Forgive me for not shaking hands. Shall we proceed?'

All this addressed in a fey voice to Jim Buckley who nodded. His attention was elsewhere.

'That's Sally,' said Harry waving his scalpel in the general direction.

It was a kind of low-rent *Silent Witness,* silent except for Sally munching on the sandwich and the scratching of her biro on a notepad. The body lay on a shiny steel table. Cato edged closer. His eyes travelled over the skin, the wounds, the stumps and the handless arm. Flipper. It didn't look human any more. But it—correction, he—once was. This shapeless lump of meat had a family somewhere. Cato would try to hold on to that thought. The smell was like an extra presence in the room. Sally seemed oblivious to it, wiping a wholemeal crumb daintily from the corner of her lips.

Dr Lewis got to work. The subject was a medium-sized male probably in the twenty to forty age-range. No obvious indications of any disease or illness. No scars, tattoos, or distinguishing birthmarks, and no obvious indications of racial origin. 'Going by the general slippage and flesh deterioration I'd estimate he's been in the water for up to a week. Sorry I can't be more precise.'

Harry examined, and Sally listed, the various wounds, mainly teeth-marks and tears. With the sandwich out of the way, Sally hopped off her stool and took some photographs.

Dr Lewis held the pale arm up, quite gently. 'Pity about the missing hand; it might have had a wedding finger, something to help us along. No such luck.'

As far as he could tell, the missing hand, right arm, and legs were probably the work of sharks. Lewis turned his attention to the neck, dragging down the magnifier on its extension arm.

'The neck hasn't been snapped like you might expect from the wrenching movement of a shark's jaw. It has been cut, or more likely sawn, perhaps with a chainsaw? A handsaw would be a lot of effort and leave more jagged markings on the bone. Not exactly my specialty but we'll get it looked at in Perth.'

Cato certainly agreed with the 'handsaw effort' part. Was it only that morning they'd been decapitating a cow in Katanning?

Lewis continued. 'So my observant friend, Dr Terhorst, would appear to be on the ball. Speaking of which, I thought he might have been with us tonight?'

He looked around the room as if Terhorst might have been hiding somewhere.

Tess looked up from writing her own notes. 'He was booked to give a talk at the Hopey Wine Club tonight. He gave his apologies, said he'd call you tomorrow.'

'A wine buff too. A man of many talents, our Dr Terhorst,' Lewis said, a touch insincerely. He made the 'Y' incision and opened the body up. Tess went pale. Cato made himself keep watching; it wasn't his first time, by any means, but it had been a while. Buckley was concentrating on Sally's calf muscles, oblivious to the carnage on the steel trolley. Lewis lifted the lungs out. Cato could see where the wiry muscularity came from. A few lung lifts every day would keep anyone in good shape.

'The lung contents rule out death by drowning,' Lewis confirmed.

He examined them further, probing with his scalpel, humming softly to himself. Cato tried to place the tune: it might have been a bit of Puccini, or Shirley Bassey. Finally Lewis glanced at Cato.

'I would say your friend was definitely dead before he went into the water.'

Cato and Tess shared a look; it seemed he was going to be around for a while longer. Lewis plucked out and squeezed what appeared to be a blood-soaked semi-deflated balloon into a plastic container. Stomach contents: pretty empty, but there were indications of rice and chicken in there. Blood, skin and tissue samples would be taken for further testing but Cato had seen enough for now. His neck prickled with something approaching excitement.

'Are you saying this is a murder, Dr Lewis?'

'Possibly; that's your job not mine. There could be any number of reasons for what we see here: accident, panic, cover-up, foul play. Anyway ...' he tapped Flipper's neck lightly with his scalpel and looked Cato straight in the eye, 'it's definitely a bit fishy.'

(From *Prime Cut*, a novel, 2011.)

# GOLDIE GOLDBLOOM

# THE ROAD TO KATHERINE

When I was five, my father dropped me off the second floor balcony of our house in Darlington. Now, I don't want you to go thinking this is one of those fake-oh made-up stories where Satan is a guy in a turban who has a thing about chopping off ladies' heads. No mate. This is God's own truth. Bloody straight up. When Satan appears in this story, he looks a hell of a lot like my dad: a bog-standard ocker in a singlet, with his gut hanging out, and no Y-fronts under his shorts.

I've never been sure if my dad dropped me on purpose. If he said, 'You're a hell of a kid, Care,' before or after he let go of my legs. I can't tell if he was a total bastard or just a dad who'd been listening to his little girl do a dummy spit for a couple of hours too long, and I don't suppose I'll ever really know. Either way, dropping me got Mum's attention.

She came blaring out of the house, hurdled the pool and was yanking my arms and legs to see if they hurt before Dad had stopped saying, 'Why'd she do a stupid thing like that?'

'Pull your finger out,' Mum called up to him, 'she's probably broken.'

She may have said this because my two front teeth were jutting through my lower lip in a way that looked unnatural.

'Call the doc,' she yelled, beer-tasting spit spraying my face.

'Why'd she jump?' he shouted back, with the concerned look of a Saint Bernard.

'He dropped you,' she hissed at me. 'He dropped you. He dropped you. Whatever he says, remember: he dropped you.'

I used to have these wicked dreams about falling.

In one version, I'd be wearing me dad's army coat, a scratchy greygreen thing with live bullets rattling round in the pockets, and as I jumped, the coat ballooned out like an umbrella opening—phwoop—and I'd float gently down like Mary Bloody Poppins. In another version, I was a Great White, swimming in a hot blue sea, and I rocked up to take a munch outta this dirty old man with mould growing down his back, only the fella turns into the bit of backyard I buried me head in and I've got double gees, the world's worst prickers, stuck right between me teeth. But the dream I'd wake up from, ice water in me veins and the echoes of screams still bouncing round the room, was the one where Dad was yelling at me not to be a sook. He had his paws around me ankles and he was shaking me over the railing like a bit of shark bait, waggling me around so the twin streamers of snot running out me conk don't end up on his person and he's saying he'll educate me not to be afraid of heights, he doesn't want any kids of his to be bloody pansies, and right then my hand almost touches him but instead grabs the railing, and a great string of me snot splats on his leg and he gets a sick look on his face that I just see out the corner of me eye as I feel his hands opening and myself hitting the edge of the concrete balcony with the side of me head, but I'm not stopping. Oh no. Not stopping there.

You'd think watching your kid take a dive off a balcony at an early age would be the kind of thing that permanently turns a man off his drink, but it was water off a duck's back with me dad. When he didn't make it home, Mum took me down to the pub and sent me in. She herself chatted with the other wifies out on the kerb. If he was blotto, he stood me up on the bar and called for bids. 'This kid's tough as nails. Jumped off the second floor balcony and *bounced*. What'll you give me for her?' he'd say, turning me around and punching my arms. The blokes at the bar reached out and pinched me bum, squeezed me muscles and handed me half-sucked butterscotch lollies covered in fluff from their pockets. 'Slave for a day?' they asked. 'Give youse a quid.' Me dad would snatch me off the bar, complaining, 'Bloody cheapskates. Mob of larrikins. This girl's a flamin' miracle. Not a mark on her. Catholic yahoos in Rome are lookin' into it. Yer can't buy something like that for a quid.' I hated the way me dad turned me around just as he said, 'Not a mark on her,' so that the jagged scar over me lip didn't show and I hated that bar and them stained-glass windows like it was a holy place, a place where you could get your sins forgiven or at least forgotten, the bartender the priest at the altar, mixing the holy spirits, and the chiming of the pint glasses the mystery, the church bells, the transformation, God help us.

I would have settled for a dad who held my hand and skipped on the way home, clicking his heels in mid-air and singing Monty Python tunes in a voice as milky and demanding as a calf's. He did all that, but the words he sang were the names of places he loved, those tin shanties beside rivers of red dirt, giant tingle trees' warm black boles filled with duff and ants and the smell of the sky, hot silver sea boiling over on a beach hidden inside the very land itself: Dumbleyung, Kojonup, Dalwallinu, Cascade, Bungle Bungle, Butty Head, Coal Miners Bay, Thirsty Point, Tittybong, Goomalling, Wave Rock, the Houtman Abrolhos; all stuff to serenade his little girl with on the way home from the pub, unaccompanied by banjo or bagpipes or anything but the snorts of his wife and his own tapping Blunnies. I would have written him off but he was too bloody likeable.

And there came a day when Mum and Dad were having a booze-up with the relatives and they—being more than half-pissed—thought it would be educational to take us kids around Australia. Of course, my dad was big on anything educational although he hadn't learned a whole lot from the last time he thought he'd teach me something. We—the kids who needed educating—were out on the balcony in our underpants and singlets, lolling about under the mosquito nets, sweating and playing Cheat by flashlight. What *we* thought was educational was turning leeches inside out down by the creek out the back of our place, and lining them up like burnt-out grey matches on the stones that edged the water. Or pinning beetles down over bull ant nests. Cripes, you could learn a lot from the way them buggers fought to stay alive.

But the grownups thought we were stunned mullets, stupid as all get-out, and that it would take a fair bit of educating to make us solid citizens, so, bright and early they loaded up the trucks and turfed us in the back. By us, I mean me and me brothers, Fred and Bill, and me half-arsed cousins, Chaz, Baz, and Flox.

Right off, I started whingeing that I wanted breakfast and me dad came back and started laying about with his belt. It was hard not to laugh, he was that predictable. The mums went in one ute, and the dads went in the other truck and there was a mad scramble when us kids realised this, all scrambling for the ute where the mums were because they had the fizzy drinks.

Dad had rigged up a tarp from each roll bar to the tailgates of the utes, half a tent where we could sleep or talk or play cards, no worries about getting sunbit. I sat on the round dooverlackie over the tyres. I was royalty. Me brother Fred lounged against the tailgate, which was typically lacklustre of him, because the latch was stuffed and it snapped open on the bumps and a year ago he'd done a belly flop onto the bitumen. Ended up with a broken collarbone. Dad knocked him around a fair bit, called him a daggy little queen, and hauled him off to shoot twenty-eights and kangaroos, without getting Fred to say more than, 'Lotta blood in them parrots, i'nt there?' Dad fair wet himself when he found out Fred had a stamp collection. A *stamp collection*, for God's sake. Fred may as well have painted a target on hisself.

Chaz was older than me, but she was albino and had glasses and a face like a festered pickle. Baz was a boy, a point he didn't hesitate to prove, although he didn't have all that much proof at the time. Little bugger couldn't have pulled a greasy stick out of a dead dog's bum. He was a prawn. Honest. And Flox was the only living brain donor in our neck of the woods. So I was the boss cocky amongst the cousins and the best at Cheat and the best at Liar and the best at Greed and everyone had to give me all their green snakes when the mums stopped at the Billabong Roadhouse and bought us lollies. The dads stopped too but they didn't buy any lollies. They were strict beer boozers.

It was at Billabong that I started thinking it would be ace if I could get half the kids over in the back of the dads' ute, because then I could stretch out, maybe even take a kip in one of the sleeping bags and, since we'd gotten up at four, this seemed like an excellent plan. I went to me mum and whined that Flox smelled like wee and so did Fred, and Chaz was too yucky to look at, with her specs and red eyes and ghost skin, and I wanted them all out. It would be better anyway because then the mums wouldn't have to watch as many anklebiters. Her eyes lit up at that, and I knew that the dads were about to become the proud new owners of a litter of mongrel puppies. She might not have been so keen on the idea if she'd seen Dad stuffing a carton of Swan Lager down next to his seat.

So I suppose it was really me own stupid fault what happened next.

It was hot as blazes and all you could see of the educational bloody bush was an orange-red blur whipping by in the triangles at the sides of the tarp. The wind came dry and mentholated, full of bushflies and the screams of cockatoos and the feathers of the twenty-eights that'd smashed on the roo bar. A hessian bag full of water hung at the tailgate and squelched as it slopped around like me dad's own belly. We'd been told that the wind cooled the water, which was bogus—it tasted like muddy tea—and we spent a lot of time spitting it at each other through our front teeth, which was fairly amusing, and then, when there was none left, drumming on the cab window, yowling about being thirsty.

'Me tongue's stuck to the roof of me bleedin' mouf.'

'I'm as dry as a dead dingo's donger.'

But the mums didn't pull over until Baz howled, 'I gotta poo. Mum! It's coming out in me daks! Mum!'

We'd just blown past the Nanuturra Roadhouse, not stopping, mainly because of the crabs Dad had picked up there a couple of years back. Mum says they weren't the edible kind, which makes sense, that far from the ocean. So Baz got pretty stinky before we pulled in at the Nerren Nerren water tanks. The station owners still hadn't twigged that tourists and truckies regularly helped themselves to their water. This far north, water was gold, diamonds and tiger meat.

Mum chucked a roll of toilet paper under the tarp, took a peek at the flyfest on Baz, and told us to get going. She told Baz to make sure to polish his date till it *shone*. I smacked aside the other contenders, grabbed the bum hankies and took off into the bush. It was a bloody hot day, the sky gone runny near the horizon. A goanna toasted himself over the sizzling red sand, his tongue moving slowly in and out of his mouth like a shellacked earthworm and smoke curling off his hide. Flies fell out of the sky and lay buzzing on the ground with heatstroke. I crawled under a bit of scrub and listened to the others spazzing about the lack of toilet paper. Baz, particularly, was doing a nutter. I kid you not. It was excellent, from my point of view, and I was a happy little Vegemite until I heard the utes start up.

'Oi!' I yelled, standing up, but the flippin' tank stand was in between me and the utes and they couldn't see me.

'Hang on!'

No one looked my way. Under the tarps, the ferals tumbled and screamed and threw cards at one another: the ace of clubs cartwheeled out and snagged on a grevillea. The utes skidded onto the track and a curtain of red dust rose behind them. I heard Dad's faint shout over the tin bucket clanking of the engines, 'Shut your gobs, youse lot!' The utes didn't stop.

I ran into the middle of the corrugated road, staring at the stakes that marked every half-mile in a straight line off to forever, and at the cloud that followed the utes and my family.

Every year, tourists die on this road. They'd be found a couple of miles from their cars, legs swollen from the lack of water, their pelts hanging in tattered red strips and they'd be eyeless. Parrots love eyes. We always carried extra jerry cans of water and petrol because the distance between roadhouses was just a bit more than one tank of juice could take you. There weren't any signs warning you about this all-important fact. The locals barely cracked a smile when foreigners in Range Rovers said to fill 'er up. Later, they'd mention that another one of those slack Pommies had carked it on up the road to Katherine, silly buggers, and no one would be surprised. No one would laugh, but they'd want to. By God, they'd want to.

I walked back to the tank stand and drank tinny yellow bore water straight from the tap before counting geckoes and termite castles and how many handfuls of the hot red dirt it took to cover my leg. Even though things were moving in there—slick, slick, slick—I buried my other leg, and then my belly, my bum and one arm. At least it kept the sun off. The stinky socks were blooming, so I picked one and, holding my nose, ate it. A snake essed across the road and tasted the damp earth under the tap. It was a king brown. They have huge black eyes and a splotch of black on their heads and my dad told me they are twelve times more poisonous than a cobra: if a king brown chomps your ankle, within five minutes you start vomiting green stuff, your gums turn purple and your heart explodes. Nice. The males are so crazy they'll hump she-snakes that were squished on the road days before.

The king brown looked in my direction and stuck out its tongue to taste the smell that was rolling off me. I saw a man like that once, in the Freo Markets; his tongue was split in two, and he could make each side move by itself. It gave me bad dreams. I wasn't afraid of the king brown though, because it wouldn't bother me unless I stepped on its tail, or ate its babies, or tried to bash in its head.

I thought that Mum and Dad would get to Carnarvon and figure out they'd left me back the track a-ways. Mum would say it was Dad who'd left me behind. Dad would say she was a dog's breakfast, and besides, she's the mum, the one who is supposed to count the kids and wipe their bums and such. Mum would tell the cops and Dad would tell the whole story down at the local pub while they waited for a truckie to bring me in. That's what I thought would happen.

Now, if I was telling you a made-up story, this is where the little lost princess would be rescued by the handsome sultan. But since I'm telling you God's own truth, I have to say that I was knackered and I fell asleep and while I was sleeping, a man driving a cement mixer pulled in to fill his water bottles with stolen water, and I woke up because I heard him calling, 'Is anyone here?'

Who he thought was hanging out at these godforsaken water tanks, I don't know. But deadset, that's what he was saying, so I stood up and said, 'Yeah. Me.'

'Shite, girlie. What you doing out here, all by yourself?' he said, scratching his armpits, right and left, with a sound like sandpaper on a block of wood. He was dressed like my dad—singlet, shorts and desert boots—but, unlike Dad, who was stunted and hairy, this bloke was tall and bald, much older, and his clothes didn't have things growing on them. He had two tiny gold hoops in one ear like Sinbad.

'Me mum and dad forgot me here, I reckon.'

'Bloody sods. When did that happen?'

'Lunchtime about,' I said, but I was already cheesed with him for calling Mum and Dad names.

The sun lay squashed near the edge of the sky and the man—Scurry, he was called—offered me a cold sausage with creamy grease on its side and a bite missing.

'Get that into you,' he said.

He said he'd take me to the police station and they'd get me sorted. We'd be there just after dark. He told me to get into the truck and I got in and dropped the sausage onto the seat between us. He stared at the banger for a moment.

Right in front of me, six polaroid photos of little kids were taped to the dash board. I leaned closer. One of the kids was an Abo, dark navy black, and her eyes were closed. She was pretty and I thought that, despite his white skin, Scurry must have some black blood in him. I touched the girl's eyes. A narrow glass vase was taped next to the photos, filled with donkey orchids and everlastings. They smelled like warm honey.

To be friendly, I said, 'You've got a lot of kids, mistah.'

'Yeah,' he said, picking up the sausage and eating it. 'I'm good at getting kids.'

'What are their names?'

'What?' he said. 'Geez. What do you care?'

Folding his sunnies, he gave me a look that'd fry spuds. I ran my fingers over the photos, played them as if they were piano keys. He took a loop of fishing line, sawed it between his teeth and a fountain of spit and rotting sausage spattered the windscreen. He splashed Old Spice on his tongue and under his arms.

He asked what my name was and when I told him Bugs, he said, 'Pig's arse,' and asked for my real name, which is about as bad as a name can be. When I told it to him, he laughed, pretty much the reaction I always get.

'Care?' he said. 'Your name is Care? I've got a bleedin' CARE package in me truck? Strewth. A CARE package from home. Everything a man could want in a little box.'

His CB radio crackled and I heard '... little girl left at the Nerren Nerren water tanks ...'

'That's me!' I said, sitting up. 'They're looking for me!'

'No drama,' he said and leaned over and turned off the radio. 'That's old news. I've got you now.'

He pushed a tape into the cassette player and Mick Jagger croaked something about laying my soul to waste, a song I happen to know because me cousin used to have all the Stones' records before she barbecued them in the backyard when she went on a religious kick.

When he smiled, just one corner of his mouth turned up. The inside of his lip was black. He didn't have any hair or eyebrows and his arms and legs had whopping bald patches. He only had a few eyelashes left. As he was driving, he'd pull out one of those and balance it on the top of the steering wheel. When that eyelash fell off, he got a cranky look on his face, and after a while he'd huff, and pull out another one.

'What are you staring at?' he said, looking quickly into the rearview and touching the place his eyebrow might have been. 'You're not exactly Marilyn Monroe yerself.'

Which was true—me being an alabaster runt in homemade floral bloomers—but at least *I* had eyelashes. I imagined him in a blonde wig and fake titties, wearing stilettos and standing over a blower, trying to hold down his flapping skirt.

'So,' he said, 'how old are you?'

'Twelve,' I said, 'in a bit. I'm eleven and a quarter.'

'Really?' he said, sitting up straighter and squeezing his thighs together. 'Twelve's a beaut age ... my dad took me to Coober Pedy to look at the opal mines when I was twelve. The miners put quartz on the opals to make them look bigger. If the quartz is on one side, it's called a doublet, see, and if it's on both sides, it's called a triplet. We stayed in a dugout, a house that's underground, to keep cool. One bloke stuck an entire crocodile skeleton on the wall of his dugout. Hung opal rings on its claws. I nicked one. I've got it here.'

Sure enough, an opal ring strangled his pinky.

'Where's your dad now?' I asked.

He didn't answer, so I asked again, and he said, 'Dumb shit fell down one of the mine shafts and I got put in a foster home,' which was a lie if ever I heard one, to make me feel bad for him.

Just before it got dark, he stopped to siphon the python and when he came back, I saw that his fly was still half open so I said, 'Flying low,' and pointed at his zipper. He flipped me a look like a rat with a gold tooth. I told him it happens to me dad all the time—he's forgetful—and it's easy to come out of the dunny and flash the family jewels at someone's old granny, so I remind him with codes. 'Flying low' was one, and so was 'LBW' which meant 'leg before wicket', or 'XYZ' which was 'examine your zipper', or 'are you afraid of heights', which I told him I was.

'I fell off the balcony when I was five, or maybe my dad dropped me. Are you afraid of heights?'

'Shut up about me fly,' he said, and plucked out one of his eyelashes.

I pointed out that his fly was still open and he stepped down hard on the pedal that makes the engine vroom, and then he zipped up.

This was the first time I had ever ridden in the front of a truck and I liked the way you can't tell you're attached to the road. It looks like you're flying. When you walk, you can see your feet touching the ground, each step gluing you down again and again but in the truck, you couldn't see any of that.

'Have you ever been on a plane?' I asked. 'Or a flying carpet?'

'There's no such thing as flying carpets. It's a load of codswallop,' he said, busy shaving the white stuff off his front teeth with his fingernail.

'Wrong again. I have a book at home that tells all about flying carpets. They gave it to me in hospital when I went to get me lip put back on after dad dropped me. It's called *The Arabian Nights* and it's the best book ever made. All the kids in hospital got books that day. It's s'posed to make you want to read, when you get your own book.'

'If my old man dropped me off the veranda, I'd have pulled his guts out of his eyeballs,' he said. 'Your dad's a danger to humanity.'

I thought of all the things I could say that would prove that Dad was a good dad, if a bit forgetful: his gentle brushing of my white hair; his reading my book to me every night—even when we'd had to haul him back from the pub—until him and me both knew every posh word; his dressing up in a sheepskin carseat cover on the way here, to try and rustle a sheep we saw near the road; the way he laughed, and called 'Gambol!' while kicking out his hind legs and wagging his bum as our lamb lunch ran away. But I couldn't say these things to Scurry, mostly because he wouldn't believe them, but also because it was hard to think about Dad that way ... like maybe he really was a good dad or at least trying to be. Also because I'd suddenly remembered the Stranger Danger class we'd been given in Grade One and how we weren't supposed to chat with people we didn't know, which it was definitely too late for, so I viciously said, 'Mum says Dad's an *excellent* dad.'

'Excellent candidate for the electric chair, more likely,' he said, and I decided to change the subject.

'Do you like to read?'

'I hate reading,' he said. 'Reading's for nongs. Who the hell would ever believe in a flying carpet except for a total nong?'

I touched the photo of the Abo girl with me big toe. She had her dad's nose. I thought I could see that. I wondered if she liked her dad. If she let him boss her around or if she imagined him in hot pants and a beehive hairdo.

'You know, Scurry, the way you got your belt, your belly looks like a humungous grandma bosom. I tell my dad all the time that if he keeps on drinking beer and eating snakes, he's going to get diabetes. The way you're going, that could happen to you too.'

'It's all muscle,' he said, patting his gut and giving me a dodgy look.

'Like fun,' I said, 'I can hear it sloshing.'

'That's the cement,' said he.

He had a head on him like a sucked mango. Dad's a bricklayer. I happen to know that cement hardens in ninety minutes and we'd been flying down the road to Katherine way longer than that. I closed my eyes and I could still see the photos of his six little kids, their faces floating and ghosty in that colourless forest.

'Do your kids like to read?'

'What kids?' he said.

Scurry was playing with my head; he thought that kind of thing was funny. Dad did too. I wanted to cry just then, but no. I'd taught Fred and Bill and Chaz and Baz and Flox my special method of not crying and it was this: You picture yourself as a two-by-four. Hitting doesn't hurt you; names don't hurt;

forgetting doesn't hurt. Whoever's pounding on you feels it when they connect, feels the little bones in their hands snapping, splinters from you stuck so far into them that they poke out the other side. Your guts beg them to hit you again, and you smile a wooden smile when they do.

So when he said, 'What kids?' I smiled.

The truck surfed through the night sky, the flick of light on the marker stakes the only thing to say we hadn't gone roaring off through the uncharted bush, and the darkness made me itchy. Scratchy in all the wrong places. It felt like something had climbed into the cab and sat down between us. The door wasn't locked. I could have jumped, flown out into that blackness if I'd wanted to, like an apple core or a beer can. If I'd had an army coat, I might have jumped. It could have worked. The coat could have opened with a phwoop and floated me down. It's London to a brick that he didn't lock the door because he thought I wasn't game for taking a ten-foot header out into the quartzy dust, but that was nothing compared to a swan dive from a second floor balcony. He just didn't know my history.

Instead of jumping, I said, 'Do you want to hear an interesting story? I could tell you the one about Sinbad.' Which I thought would interest a bloke with earrings.

'No,' he said.

'It's in my book.'

'Listen, squid, I wouldn't be so chuffed about that bloody book if I was you. You only got it because your old man chucked you off a balcony.'

'He might not have dropped me. I might have jumped. I think I did jump.'

'*If* you jumped,' he said, 'why'd you land on your head?'

'You're yucky,' I said and I twisted and kicked him as hard as I could in the place that everyone says hurts the most, the toyshop under the awning, and it was squashy there and he screamed, 'You liddle bugger!' and grabbed my ankle, reeling me in as the truck swerved to the left and I bashed my head on something. The drying concrete squealed and metal parts I didn't know the names of ranted as the right side of the truck rose and stars spun down into the window. I thought we'd roll over. I thought we'd have mushy grey brainstuff on our faces, and broken glass for diamond rings, but Scurry didn't let the truck escape. It bumped back onto all its wheels, and the glovebox sprang open and his polaroid camera fell out in me lap. Black pearls of sweat shone on the camera, smelling of motor oil, trembling before they slid down and bled into me cotton bloomers. I put the camera back, next to the duct tape and the filleting knife, and shut the little door with a click that made Scurry flinch.

'You're a bastard,' I said, watching his face in the black reflection of the side window.

'The only bastard you know is the one who dropped their kid off a balcony,' he said, grinning like a shot fox, and the truck hit a marker. The stake flew up past my window, a comet, or a falling star, just a blur inside my eyeballs.

'They should have locked him up,' he said. 'Why didn't they?'

I didn't want to talk about my dad anymore with this mangy bloke with no eyelashes, so I stuck my fingers in my ears and said, 'Woo woo woo woo.' Another marker whipped up, hit the silver bulldog on the front of the truck and shattered.

He yanked my hand away from my ear and said, 'I bet you told them you fell.'

Which was the truth. Straight up. I lied to the doctor who asked me how I fell, and I lied to the nurses and, what the heck, I lied to Scurry too. I'm the queen of Liar. But I put me fingers back in me ears and closed me eyes and whispered 'Woo woo' like it was a spell, some kind of voodoo prayer that could turn me into someone else. After listening to me for a while, he cranked up old Mick, and lay another eyelash on the steering wheel.

'Scurry,' I said, 'I could tell you a different story. Something you'll like.'

He didn't say anything for a long time.

'I could tell you about Scheherazade. She's the towelhead who told all the stories in me book, a thousand and one stories, one every night.'

'Why?' he asked, glancing at me and his eyes looked huge and black. He bunged on the brakes and pulled off the road. I didn't have the foggiest where we were. Somewhere dark, in the back of beyond. He opened his door and told me to get out. The wind from the coast was strong enough to blow a dog off its chain and it thudded in my ears, blew the hairs in me eyebrows backwards, whipped me eyelashes against my dry eyeballs. I could barely suck in a breath, the air rushed by so fast. A sheet of sand peeled off and snapped a few feet from the ground. My shorts rippled, my shirt ballooned, hair lashed my face. I felt my body lifting, my feet barely touching the ground.

At last, he asked, 'Why did she tell so many of them stories?'

He held my wrist so I wouldn't blow away. I could smell his strong penicillin smell and the Old Spice on his tongue. The polaroid camera, shoved by the wind, hit me, and it smelled like a gun after it goes off. He put his sunnies on.

'Just listen,' I said. 'There was once a wicked king, who got married to a different girl every night, and every morning, he'd cut off her head.'

'Hah!' he laughed, '*Excellent.*'

'I told you you'd like it. It's your kind of story. Scheherazade offered to get married to him. All the other girls was forced, but she offered. She told her sister to come in the night, and then she told her a story, and the shah began to listen too, because she was a dinkum storyteller. Right when the sun come up, she stopped. She wouldn't tell the end.'

'Did he kill her?' he asked and I smelled the old fish stink of the knife.

'No. The shah wanted to hear the end of the story, so he let her live and she come to him the next night, and that night, she done the same thing. Told a story, but not the end.'

'For a thousand and one nights.'

'Yeah. And he let her live because he liked her stories.'

His voice floated to me, soft in the darkness. 'They must have been good stories.'

'I could tell you a good story,' I said.

'Go on then,' he said. 'Tell me.'

The wind shouting through the casuarinas, the strips of hanging bark pattering against the gum trees, the boobooking of the tawny frogmouths, everything, stilled, and the bush breathed deeply, waiting.

(From *You Lose These*, short fiction, 2011.)

# DEBORAH ROBERTSON

# THE TRANSFER OF TRACY GREEN

I had the sharp muscles of captivity but deep down I felt weak. My hair was its natural nothing again. I was untanned and undecorated and since the smoking ban, with regard to all comforts, I was clean.

Who was I? I was Tracy Green. Thirty-two years old. Prisoner 2159.

Species: *Saltwater Suburban Girl.*

Habitat: Brick and tile, cul-de-sac, khaki grass.

Conservation Status: Not rare, under no threat whatsoever of extinction.

Appearance: Five foot five. Skin: light olive. Bone structure that allows hair to be worn short, although in captivity the cut is rough. Differs in this respect from others in the species with bigger hair. Amber eyes with a touch of cat, big feet, long toes. Long fingers that facilitate the wearing of many large rings, sometimes leading to further classification of the subspecies *Saltwater Bohemian Suburban Girl,* this subspecies characterised by yearning, a dream for another way to be.

Note: the subspecies classification of Tracy Green has never remained stable. Her taste for tight black jeans and free-form dancing has sometimes led to classification as *Saltwater Rock Chick Suburban Girl*, but depending upon the cut of the jeans and the style of head movement in the dance, at other times *Saltwater Bogun Suburban Girl* has been more accurate.

It is important to observe that in captivity the wearing of a uniform eliminates the need for fine classification, rendering all prisoners homogenous, and all skins sallow.

I've thought hard about how to describe to you what it's like being in prison, and I've decided that really the only way is to ask you to try to imagine something.

It's an airport I want you to imagine, and you have to imagine you're travelling alone. You've reached your departure lounge and there's been a delay, things are going to take a while, so choose a seat, burgundy or bottle green, and get used to it. Note how far away the rest of the world feels—the place you've left and the place you're trying to get to—there's no choice but to give in to the moment. It's a child's waiting, a child's submission, that's asked of you. Can you put aside your book or newspaper and try to feel this, how infantile you've become?

Study the people around you now. You'll see it in your own face when you go to the toilet and glance up from washing your hands: you look less than yourself. You look dull, you feel grey. It's something to do with the waiting. You'd gone so fast to get there, and now it's just the stop, the hanging around, stasis. All the blood and piss in the body slows, life congeals on the face. The lovely become plain, the plain become ugly, the ugly become the ones you hope to God you're not going to have to sit next to when at last you board that plane.

You would never have chosen these fellow travellers; you know this and they know it too. It's partly why no one looks at each other while they wait—these are the people you might perish beside on route to wherever you're going. The people you might try to save, or be saved by, or sacrifice in order to save your own life.

Nothing you do now will make a jot of difference to the waiting: it will go on and on. It might get so bad that you want to argue with the girl in the ponytail who microphones the messages of more waiting, but argument won't help, there's no chance in hell of anything changing.

You're going to be asked to throw your phone in the bin now (the big grey one over there, the one with the grubby lid). I'll ask nicely, but I will only ask once. Throw away your books and magazines while you're there. You might get them back later, I don't know, it isn't up to me, but you can keep your iPod, for the moment, if you're good.

Now we're getting somewhere. With the imagining, that is, not with the waiting. Time is still ticking slowly by. In this next step, you will need to imagine that the departure lounge is being cordoned off. Any good strong rope will do, or crime scene tape, as long as it encloses everyone there: the girls clipping about in high heels with their walkie-talkies (to remind you that you are an infant there is baby-talk), the men bustling in busy-person, day-glo jackets, the passengers waiting on the chairs, the passengers who are standing because they are stoic or because they cannot abide being wedged between the bodies of strangers in rows of seats when so much wedging and rowing is still ahead of them.

Everyone is together, and now you must take out the men—just lift the rope and they can slip under it. The children will have to go next, the ones who are old enough to walk, or waddle. Even in imagination it's no simple thing, this moment of taking the children away. For some children there will be men waiting outside the cordon, others will be passed amongst strangers, but the rest must wander off into the world alone.

We'll have to wait for a while now, for the women to settle.

Some will need to find a wall to turn their faces to, but those afraid of what else might be taken from them will choose to remain in their seats. It's only the women with the walkie-talkies who swing into action: clipping around in their new uniforms designed by those big names Hip & Shit, communicating with the static coming through from the outside world, sniffing the fear and liking it.

Imagine the thoughts of the women against the walls or sitting together, caught in this mysterious loop of time, in a place between leaving and arriving. Imagine their clothes turning burgundy and bottle green, their feet swelling, growing heavy, massing with roots, binding them to this place.

Remember the rope, the crime scene tape? Pull it tight now. Electrify it, so that no one gets out alive. And there you have it at last: prison, as close as I can get.

There are just two more things you'll need to do to complete the picture, make it real. You will have to imagine that the airline is a budget one, because nearly every woman there is on the bones of her arse. And a third of the women—even though you might never have seen such a thing in your life—you must colour a third of the women black.

Gloriana Women's Prison had been built in the 1950s. It had low, red brick buildings with concrete verandahs, demountables, and kidney-shaped flowerbeds stuffed with yellow roses. Apart from the ten-foot fence looped with razor wire, there are probably some primary schools still like it today.

They did a study at Gloriana once, about self-harm. People asked us questions and there were forms to fill out. I've never been any good with forms—I look at boxes and start to panic. I can't afford to panic, and I wasn't a cutter myself anymore, so I just wrote in big letters TAKE DOWN THE RAZOR WIRE. If the people who had power over us didn't have the imagination to consider our imaginations, why bother?

Muster on an average day at Gloriana was around one hundred. You're probably surprised by that number. You thought there were more bad women than that? You thought wrong, and it's not that there are more women out in the world who haven't been caught. It's just that women are no good at getting away with crime. And I'm sorry to break the news to you, but it's not that women are better people than men either; we just know this about ourselves, carry the knowledge stamped inside us: we're odds on to get caught, or even turn ourselves in, and knowing that, except in cases of madness or desperation—which is most of the cases here—why would you try?

If you're waiting for me to tell you about my crime, then you should know that I won't—it's an arrangement I have with the person I harmed. I was quick to admit my guilt, but it was a long time before everything my victim had lost became as real to me as my own losses.

The world expects remorse, and it's right to because without it there's too much terror. But the world wants remorse served fast, like food and sex, while really remorse is slow. People like to talk about punishment and penance, God and being good. Confession and apology taste sweet to them, but remorse, heeding none of this, continues its slow work. Remorse destroys part of you and replaces it with part of your victim. Remorse gnaws tiny holes in you and vomits up an essence of your victim to fill them, and it does this until you no longer know where you begin and your victim ends. That's really where you started from in the first place, when you committed your crime, only now what you feel for your victim has changed. Now you and your victim are together, forever, for the purpose of some sense on this earth.

But I'm afraid you'll become bored if I don't tell you about my crime. You'll be disappointed in me and you'll wander away before I've told you my story. So let me say this: on a scale from good to bad, one to ten, I'm about a six point five. Some would say seven. I have perhaps more than the average amount of violence in me, but given slightly different circumstances in my life, I might have had none.

I was leaving Gloriana, after years. I'd been medicated, educated. I had been evened-out and adjusted. I was being moved from maximum to minimum security, a prison called Dryandra, where I would be prepared for release. If anyone knew exactly how long that preparation would take, they weren't telling me. 'It's up to you,' they said.

I can't remember when Do As You're Told was replaced by It's Up To You. Maybe it was set down in my file as the day my shame should end and rehabilitation begin, but the change took place without warning or explanation, like when fruit and yoghurt replaced rice pudding at dinner—having to get used to something new because it was supposed to be good for you. Anyway, it didn't take long to work out that it was really only a slight modification in treatment, and now the rule was It's Up To You To Do As You're Told.

I didn't like Corrections Officer Mulholland. On April 26 2008, the day I had waited for—my last at Gloriana—it was CO Mulholland who first spoke of Elizabeth Fritzl.

'Did you hear about that guy who locked up his daughter and all those kids she had?' she said, drawing a ChapStick across her mouth.

There were five of us at the table, bent over breakfast bran and Sudoku.

'Where?' asked Ursula. Ursula had been undone by crystal meth.

'Not sure, Switzerland maybe?' said Mulholland. 'I can't

remember, somewhere near there—he kept her in a dungeon for twenty-four years.'

'It was Austria,' I said, not looking at anyone. I'd seen the story on the late news—I had media privileges some of the others didn't—and I had fallen asleep with his face in my head.

The moment the story began you knew it was going to be bad, but when Joseph Fritzl's photo appeared on the screen the doors of hell flew open. Although his face sagged, it wasn't just the drapery of age, but of flesh that'd had too much of everything it ever wanted. He had vicious, hooked eyebrows over pale, pitiless eyes and a lolly-pink mouth decorated with a small moustache. It was a face icy with vanity, the face of an aged porn star, and it was just as well his guilt seemed beyond doubt because it would be difficult to convince any human being with nerve endings that it wasn't.

I didn't want to give my feelings away to Mulholland as she stood over us, but at the same time I knew the danger in this story and I didn't want her to take control of it. Slowly, without elaboration, I told the others what I knew. I told of rape in the dungeon: seven children born, one dead, three taken above ground to be raised on lies, the others who grew hunched and stuttering. I told of no sun, no air, mother and children digging soil with their hands to make bigger their own prison. The more I told, the more it began to sound like a fairytale, and like a fairytale, it sliced deep.

I had learned how to read the smallest of signs in that place, the hardening of the pupils in another woman's eyes—black oil to black coal—and the trouble it meant for her, or us. As I told the story I studied my listener's eyes.

'What about the girl's mother?' asked Ursula.

'She says she never knew a thing,' said Mulholland, having her moment at last.

Time was up and we all stood. As we filed out to our places

of work and study, I watched Mulholland join another group of women and begin the story again, better informed now. I saw her later, when my shift in the bakery began, and she was telling it there too. All day she moved through the prison, keeping her lips moist, the story juicy. She was like a person strolling through the rooms of a house, pouring petrol, striking matches—by lockdown the place was on fire.

I saw it in the faces of the other women. I heard it in their voices, and in the clash of cutlery in the cafeteria. The story of Elizabeth Fritzl was moving through everyone: the sadists, the unlucky, the kicked, used, broken and overwhelmed, the unsound and the terribly sad.

It was in the air like gas. It smelled hot, blue. The weakest part of everyone was exposed, belly-up. By then we all knew what Elizabeth Fritzl had looked like, twenty-four years ago, when she was first entombed. Fresh, pretty, lit. She showed no signs of trouble, but trouble there must have been. No one believed her Daddy had been a nice one until the day she helped him install the door to her own cell and he held the ether-soaked rag to her face. She hadn't been imprisoned with earlier happy-Daddy memories to ease her horror, twenty-four years was not the sum of it.

All day I watched the shadows of the Fritzl family moving over the prison walls. When I was finally locked in my cell that night I didn't want to read or watch television. The prison was never silent or dark, but I could think at last.

Had the day really happened the way I thought? Maybe the story was just another piece of news, a bit grislier than most, and the other women had only batted it lightly back and forth, gossiped. What if it was just my mind again, the mind that had committed my crime?

Had the story thrown open the cellar door in every woman there, or had I imagined it? And if I had imagined it, did that mean I was not ready for Dryandra yet—and when would I ever be?

It had been such a long time since I'd hurt myself, since the song of cutting had sung to me. I lay down on my narrow bed and closed my eyes against the fear of myself. Cutting would end the confusion in my head, not knowing if my mind and the way it understood the world was real. I ached to go deep, to know at least this about myself, that I was flesh and blood.

In the morning there would be forms to fill out, panic boxes. There'd be a final visit to the nurse for a health check, and to make sure I wasn't smuggling contraband in my ears or my arse. I could think of nowhere to cut myself that wouldn't show—knowing that once I started I'd have to see bone. Any mark the nurse found on me would mean that I wasn't going to Dryandra.

Not that day, not in the near future.

So what did I want more—cutting or leaving? This was life as I hadn't known it in a long time, balanced on a slender thread belonging only to me. I opened my eyes and saw the Fritzl shadows playing over the walls, stalking on stilts across the ceiling. I counted the shadows: father, daughter, children alive and dead. But where was *she*? Where was Elizabeth's mother?

Did she see nothing, hear nothing—did she have no other sense with which to ask? Was she busy baking apfelstrudel, feeding her man? Or did she doubt her own mind, like I did, and in doubting had she handed it to her husband for safe keeping?

I was hauled to my feet. There wasn't enough room to pace, to stride my anger out, so I turned tight circles, my arms wrapped around me. It hurt, this sudden fury. I tried to breathe into the centre of it, but my breathing was sharp, ragged, there was too much fuel in me, the fire just burned on.

I had promised myself that I would never think of it

again—the knife with which I'd committed my crime. The finest blade in the set, wet with potato juice, waiting on the kitchen bench. There were daydreams and there were nightmares, but I knew daymares too, so I stretched out on the bed and allowed my mind to pick up that knife.

I was in a kitchen again, but this time it was the kitchen of Mrs Fritzl. She was vivid and three-dimensional when I'd finished making her, although fashioned crudely: I gave her a floral, flour-smudged apron, currant eyes in doughy flesh, a tight-stitched mouth. I built her huge, a shelf of bosom and triangle legs balanced on tiny feet. I put the tiny feet into girly shoes—Mary Janes—and then I came up from behind and stabbed her.

I stabbed close to her heart. I ran the knife like a sewing machine needle up and down her back. My neck hurt so I stabbed her there too, and when she toppled I leapt on her chest. I didn't imagine blood because I didn't care about that. It was only the yielding material of her I cared about, the in and the out. She didn't have to die, I only wanted to give her something to think about, and when all my anger was gone, I stopped.

I undressed in the dark, pulled back the covers and slipped into bed. There was no confusion in me now, only the same small guilt and sadness and peace I felt after I masturbated. I felt no need for that, and it was my last night in Gloriana.

The next morning everything took longer than it should have because Elizabeth Fritzl was still moving through the prison. The nurse was late to see me because there were women with more urgent needs, and the COs were busy hosing down brushfires. I was put in my cell with my two small plastic bags of possessions, and I waited.

Everyone was always saying that Gloriana was going to be

knocked down, so after a while no one made a fuss when we wrote on the walls. *Life has to be lived forwards, but it can only be understood backwards.* I'd written that, or at least Soren Kierkegaard had. And I'd written lists of things that I hoped lay ahead of me, at Dryandra and beyond. *Indian Ocean sunset. Trust myself.*

I thought about the woman who would live in this cell after me, and what these words would mean. I wondered if she was already committing her crime, fitting it into her day along with the shopping, or if, like me, she was soon to wake to the hours that would change her forever.

It was after lunch when someone at last came to get me.

'You're going to have to change out of that trackie,' said the CO, looking me up and down.

'Colour doesn't suit me?'

'Ha-ha,' she said.

I hated it when people said that. Either you thought something was funny or you didn't, but you didn't have to be mean about it. 'And what am I supposed to wear now?'

'Don't know,' said the CO. 'They've got something waiting for you, I think.'

What they had waiting for me were the clothes I'd been wearing the day I arrived at Gloriana, the ones I'd worn to court. I was led into the area where all those years ago I had been stripped and searched. I got out of my hoodie and T-shirt okay, but by the time I reached my track pants I was shaking so much I couldn't stand.

'It might be easier if you took off your shoes first?' said the CO, all sarcastic.

I sat on the bench with my pants around my knees and unlaced my runners. Maybe if I'd let myself imagine this day I wouldn't be having so much trouble. But I'd been strict with myself, tried never to think of time.

'Am I taking my shoes?' I asked the CO, who was politely looking elsewhere, fiddling with her keys.

'I dunno, I guess so.'

'Could you find out?' I stood in front of her in my bra and knickers, challenging her to look, taking this small measure of power over her, that I wasn't fat.

I heard her discussing it outside in the corridor as I pulled on the skirt and blouse. They were much too big for me now. I had dressed to my lawyer's instructions. She'd presented me to the justice system looking like any young, clean, unfashionable office worker who had just destroyed her own and somebody else's life.

'You keep the shoes,' the CO said when she returned to the room, and then she looked at me and stopped. 'Oh,' she said.

'Oh, what?' I asked, my feet cold on the concrete floor.

'Oh, you look like such a baby in that.'

I looked down at the little yellow flowers on the blouse and the crushed pleats of the skirt and my eyes filled with tears. I felt sorry for trying to make her feel bad about her weight.

'It's freezing outside,' she said. 'Haven't you got tights or something?'

'It was summer when I came in.'

'Okay, hurry up, then, let's get you on the road.'

There were two police officers waiting when we got back to the office. Constable Rogers was maybe a bit younger than me. Perky, sporty, jokey—I knew the type. As far as I'm concerned, there are two types of Australian female: those who have played netball, and those who would never even consider it. And those two types can't ever get along, because their values prevent it.

But Constable McDermott was tall with a smooth, wistful face. He had broad, expressive hips, so that his gun in its holster looked no more threatening than a taffeta bow. It took no imagination at all to see how good he'd look in a long satin dress. I'd forgotten this, that on the outside there were men who looked like women—I'd forgotten about surprises with no fear in them, perhaps even a smile.

'Mind your head,' said Constable McDermott, as he helped me into the back of the car. Both of them sat in the front—that was my next surprise—like I was just a regular passenger, even a client.

All the time I'd been in Gloriana I hadn't really known where the prison was located. I'd fitted myself into a corner of the van that delivered me from court, and not looked. I'd been told that the prison was out of town—where they prefer prisons to be—and a visitor had said it was a two CD drive to get there. Not understanding where I was in relation to the city where I'd been born and raised just made things lonelier, as if we all existed on a prison planet in an outer galaxy, far away from Mother Earth.

I closed my eyes until I knew we were through Gloriana's gates, and when I opened them there was an empty bitumen road, brown scrub, rainclouds on the horizon, and the backs of the constables' heads. I wanted to drink in the world and know this time where I was going, but I also had to protect myself from the moment when the journey ended and the world was gone again. I tried to look at things as if I were peeking out of a blindfold, which worked while it was only the three of us and the sky and scrub, but then we turned in to a road with trucks and a flower stall and a sign that read *strawberries ahead.*

'Are you cold?' said Constable McDermott, turning on the heater.

The traffic thickened and there were car colours I'd never seen before, burnt orange, peacock blue, a hurting green. As we waited at a set of traffic lights I tried to understand what I was feeling: there was something else I'd forgotten about the world that was more than just its small surprises. All around us drivers were behaving themselves, half an eye on the police car, looks of pretending.

I remembered this long thin road, its four squashed, potholed lanes of traffic. Times had been good, even in prison you knew that, but only the cars gave any sign. I watched carefully, my mind seeking whatever it was about the world that was harder than a surprise to grasp. It had something to do with the mystifying clash of existences out here, how everything shared the same time and space, Elizabeth Fritzl in her dungeon, *strawberries ahead*, and nothing to explain the unfairness, nothing to help with the hurt.

It was good to see the sad old motels and the different shapes of buildings now, all the new apartments had something geometric going on. But I was glad I was only taking a little sip of the world on my way to Dryandra. I wasn't prepared for any of this, the way the world looked so sharp and decided, so sure of itself, and my mind, not certain of anything.

I would do my best at Dryandra, in minimum security. I'd take everything it offered, learn what I could. I knew how ready I'd have to be when I was finally free in this world of no security at all.

# DAVE WARNER
# JASPER'S CREEK

The report of shots fired came from some adventurous tourists who had foregone ceiling fans, sachets of hair conditioner, soft sheets and high priced grog to brave bush, crocs and mosquitoes and thereby experience the True Australia. If he'd ever had any idea what the True Australia was, Detective Inspector Daniel Clement had long since admitted defeat in capturing it. So far as he could tell True Australia was Maoris and Sri Lankans singing their lungs out on TV to impress a bunch of overseas judges to win a career singing American songs someplace other than here. True Australia definitely wasn't the front bar of the Picador late on Saturday night. At least he hoped it wasn't. Yet people had it in their heads that drunk losers breaking pool cues over one another's heads was a link in a chain that stretched all the way back to Anzac Cove.

'True Australia.'

He gave a bitter grunt and pushed the accelerator flat. He wished the Net had never been invented. He longed for a return to the days of high-cost air-travel when only the wealthy could afford to see another country. Then these adventurous tourists from Tokyo or Oslo or Rio would never have had a clue about the Kimberley region in the north-west of the Great Southland and he wouldn't have to worry about shots fired and the possibility somebody was illegally taking crocodiles, a job that should have been left to Fisheries or Parks and Wildlife but they were thin on the ground, the call had come to the station and the tourists were probably tweeting now about their 'brush with death'. Somebody had to take the trouble to check it out. He could have left it till the uniforms were able to take a look but they were all run off their feet. Hagan and Lalor were still hours inland sorting out the tribal stoush, di Rivi and Restoff had their hands full processing a grand final party that had got out of hand. As for his fellow detectives, his sergeant Graeme Earle was off fishing and his junior, Josh Shepherd, tied up in court on the domestic violence case so, senior detective or not, he was left to do the dirty work.

As well, his tooth continued to flare, and the bloke with the hammer had been at it again before six, none of which helped his disposition. He forced himself to take a deep breath. Phoebe had taken to referring to him as Mr Cranky though he had no doubt the words were her mother's. Marilyn still hadn't forgiven him for transferring here. 'Chasing us' had been the phrase she'd used. Marilyn was angry because she believed he'd made the kind of sacrifice for their daughter he never would have for her when they were together. She was probably right but he would always love her, part of him anyway, the part you couldn't explain any more than the part that of him that wedged itself between them like a crowbar. And she wasn't snow white, this wasn't all at his feet. She hadn't married that turkey, Brian, yet. Maybe Brian hadn't asked or maybe she treated him the same way as she'd treated him, like he never quite measured up. If her old man had still been alive Clement would have had an ally. Nick might have died a rich pearl farmer but he started as a bloody boat mechanic. Geraldine was the problem, she always had been. She loved to play the Lady of the Manor and Clement had been the stablehand never good enough for her daughter. It had taken a dozen years, but Marilyn had eventually synched with her mother on that, though sometimes Clement toyed with the idea she might be having second thoughts, might have at least understood her role in their demise and that's why she hadn't walked down the aisle again.

He had calmed now. This wasn't so bad, getting out of the office and away from petty crap a rookie could handle. The low, dry scrub either side of the road reminded him of those baking hot days when, as a boy, he'd played at being a soldier sliding towards his imagined enemy. Experience had taught him the enemy was generally not where you thought or even who you thought. Marilyn was happy to overlook the fact he'd grown up here too. Sure his lineage was far less grand, no pearl farm, just a caravan park his mum and dad worked up from scratch but this had been his home for fifteen years. He had almost escaped it.

Almost.

The turn-off was up ahead. Australians signposted their roads in the same laconic style they spoke. For a hundred years nobody visited Australia except English cricket teams or Russian circus performers, and no circus performers or cricketers ever bothered to come to places like this. So signs were a waste of time. If you weren't local you wouldn't be here, simple as that. If you weren't local and you were here, you shouldn't be. You were a freak, not the kind of person desired and therefore not to be encouraged by signage.

Many things might have changed but that attitude was buried so deep in the national psyche that it persisted. Unless you knew there was a track about to come up on your left that led down to the waterhole you'd eventually be in Darwin still looking for the non-existent sign that said Jasper's Creek.

But Clement knew.

He braked and turned easily down the wide dirt track. A

four-wheel drive was as necessary as insect repellent up here. Clement passed a bullet-riddled Parks and Wildlife sign showing a crocodile and the word DANGER. They couldn't signpost a road but the odd spectacular death by croc had put the wind up the bureaucrats in the Tourism Department enough to get every little creek for five hundred k covered. He could see rust around the edges of the bullet holes so he knew they weren't anything to do with the shots reported as coming from here in the early hours. Over the phone the tourists had given him a precise location for where they were when they heard the gunshots so Clement drove towards a waterhole he'd always known as Jasper's. Who the hell Jasper was, nobody had been able to tell him. The waterhole wasn't named on any map, it was too small down in mangrove territory. The bush was denser here, with paperbark, blackboy even a few big gums. Clement pulled up at the point where the car-trail narrowed.

No matter how long you lived up here, you never got used to the dry blast of hot air that hit you the moment you stepped out of air conditioning. Clement felt it now: suffocating, morbid, unfriendly heat. He began walking through bush toward the creek bank. Flies greeted him like a lost king.

Having read up thoroughly about the nocturnal habits of crocs, the tourists had slept on the roof of their campervan. It was a practice Clement didn't recommend. Already since he'd transferred, he'd dealt with two incidents of people falling from their perch during the night and cracking bones in the dirt below. One bloke was pissed and had simply overbalanced. The other had woken up at dawn, forgotten where he was, and rolled straight off the roof. Better to simply scrunch up in your car or move further away from the water. Still, they'd been wise to be cautious. There'd recently been reports of a large croc in the area that had taken a pig-dog.

It took only a few minutes to find the car tracks and the broken scrub from where the tourists had driven out. According to them, the shots had come from the west side of the creek but as it was night, they'd seen nothing and simply hightailed it out of there. Clement didn't blame them. He suspected it was probably a couple of drunk hoons firing at the stars but it could have been some dickhead after a croc. Close to the creek the trees bent in and leaned over the dark water, boughs sprawled across the muddy bank like a party-goer who'd never made it home; the light was dappled, the smell of rotting weeds and dead wood that brought to mind dragonflies and mosquitoes. Here Clement was extremely careful. Coming out of the bright light into this shadowy grove, your eyes took time to adjust and you could literally trip over a big croc lazing in its muddy bed. He made sure the logs near the bank were logs, then advanced close enough to be able to look west to the other bank, a distance he estimated might be a swimming pool and a half, say eighty metres. His first scan registered nothing out of the ordinary but as he looked back the other way he sensed rather than saw something wasn't right. His focus narrowed to a shag levitating above the water but without its wings extended. Closer inspection revealed it was sitting on something curved and silver, the bottom of an upturned tinny. It was in shallow water right near the edge of the opposite bank but, despite the proximity, there was no way Clement was swimming across. Foreboding thudded in Clement's chest, not a salvo, not a flurry, just one solid thump. He started around to the other side of the creek.

'Anybody there?'

His words spun around the empty space and slapped him.

No reply.

The bush was thick and spikey through here. Sharp, stiff foliage poked into his neck and the backs of his legs, tangled branches scratched his arms. It was as if the bush were saying, keep away, leave me alone, I don't want you here, like the absence of signage was its choice. Even pushing as quickly as he could it took him a good ten minutes to circumnavigate the creek and get to the opposite side from where he'd started. His position now was directly in line with the partly submerged tinny, about twenty-five metres away back in the bush. A gap in the foliage surrounding the creek at this point meant there were no trees obstructing his line of sight. He guessed this might be why you'd launch your tinny from here. No outboard motor was visible on the tinny and alarms bells sounded that fraction louder. Every tinny up here had some kind of motor. He called out again but heard only the ghost of his own voice. He continued on his arc, sideways rather than down to the water because he was after the vehicle that had carried the tinny, shoving his way through a tight screen of bush, sweating like a pig. About ten metres on, in a small clearing was an early model Pajero, the driver door open. A low hum turned him around. A one-man tent was pitched directly behind. It looked like somebody had poured a sack of tea over it: bush flies, thousands of them. Off the nearest tree, Clement snapped a small branch and waved its dead leaves around near the tent. The flies scattered long enough for him to recognise they'd been feasting on blood, quite a deal of it from the looks, tacky, not fresh but relatively recent, over the nylon tent and in the dark earth.

Steeling himself, Clement flipped back the tent flap.

Another dense army of flies. Fifty or so launched themselves at his eyes and nostrils, the rest remained undisturbed, clumped on what had once been a cooked chicken. Apart from a sleeping bag, and a couple of utensils and plastic drinking cup, nothing else was in the tent. No blood from what he could see. If the blood on the tent was from an animal killed on a hunt, there was so sign of the carcass. His guts tightened fractionally. Something bad had happened to somebody here.

'Hello. Is there anybody here?'

He yelled it as loud as he could but all tone was flattened by the vast emptiness around him. He yelled again. And again. There was no response. He turned his attention to the vehicle, put it at eight to ten years old, small dents in the body and paintwork, scratches spanning a few years. His guess: either bought second-hand in this condition cheap, or the owner was a drinker who preferred to save his money for grog. The roof bore racks for transporting the tinny. Through the back window he could see fishing rods and tackle, a bucket, esky, various crap, old towels and a tarp. Making sure to touch nothing he peered down at the back seat. A pair of wading boots, shoes, three empty cans of VB. He moved to the open driver door and was surprised to find the key in the ignition. Closer inspection showed the lights were switched to on but the car headlights weren't illuminated. He carefully twisted the key in the ignition with as little grip as possible already aware fingerprints might be important.

Not a kick, flat battery his diagnosis. The glove box was open and disturbed. In the crack where the hinges sat was a live cartridge, twenty-two by the looks. There was another on the floor where it might have spilled. No weapon though.

It was looking more and more like a crime-scene. No blood in the car. No obvious sign of more than one person, no women's clothing, anything like that. Clement slowly circumnavigated the vehicle. A bumper sticker extolled the virtues of Broome Anglers.

Clement used his phone to take photos of the scene and record the car's number plate and odometer setting. A phone burst into life somewhere close by. Generic ringtone. Clement tracked the sound to the dirt a few metres from the edge of the creek. Using his shirt over his fingers, Clement carefully picked up an older model smart phone. Number Withheld flashed on the screen. Clement answered.

'Hello?'

No answer but somebody was on the other end.

'This is Detective Inspector Daniel Clement ...'

The line went dead. Clement stared at the phone. His police car was equipped with a computer that would enable him to trace the Pajero plates but to get back to it through the bush was going to take another twenty minutes slog. He scrolled through the phone's last calls dialled. The most recent was identified as 'Rudi'.

He dialled, using his own phone.

Voicemail. A man, foreign accent, something European. 'I'm not available. Leave a message.'

Clement left a brief message asking Rudi to call him. He scrolled to the next entry which was labelled 'Club'. Clement had never been inside the Anglers Club but he'd passed it often enough, a small modern brick building at the industrial end of town, so indistinguishable it could as easily have been a public dunny or Scout headquarters. Broome was a small town and he doubted there would be more than fifty members of the Anglers. He gave it a try. The phone rang for some time. He was about to give up when a woman answered.

'Anglers.'

'This is Detective Inspector Daniel Clement.' He ran through his spiel. He was at an abandoned vehicle he thought might belong to one of the members. After eliciting the woman's name was Jill he described the car.

'Just a sec,' Jill said. He heard her calling to somebody in the background. She came back on. 'Sounds like Dieter's.'

'Dieter who?'

A further bout of offline consultation was followed by 'Schaffer. Don't ask me how you spell it. Is everything okay?'

That was the question, wasn't it?

Apparently Dieter Schaffer was about sixty-five, retired and unmarried. He generally fished alone. The only number they had on him was the mobile. He lived way out on Cape Leveque Road somewhere. Jill didn't know who Rudi was. Clement got off the phone and considered his options. His gut said it was a probable crime scene but there could be many explanations for what he'd found. Schaffer could have accidentally shot or cut himself, then called Rudi or some other mate to come get him. Clement rang Derby Hospital, and got Karen, who had made it abundantly clear to him several times that there was always a bed ready for him there, with her in it. Karen was late forties and it showed in her face but she had the taut body of a woman half her age.

'You finally asking me out?'

Clement sidestepped. 'You have a Dieter Schaffer there? Sixty-five, German accent, emergency admittance most likely?'

'We got a twenty-something idiot who blew himself up with his barbecue gas bottle.'

'Anybody admitted with any sort of gunshot or other wound the last twenty hours?'

'No. And you still haven't answered my first question.'

'I'm not dating.'

'I'm not asking for a date.'

He had to extricate. 'I'll buy you a beer at The Banksia.'

'She's not coming back to you, Dan. Sooner you understand that the better off you'll be.'

'Thank you, Karen.'

'My pleasure. I'll call you if Mr Schaffer turns up here.'

He'd never slept around on Marilyn. Once or twice he'd kissed women, a greeting or farewell, felt that jolt, knew that if he wanted it, anything was on the table but he always pulled back, no matter how bad it was with Marilyn at the time. He was never sure if this was any testament to his morality, he liked to think so, but maybe he just wanted the high ground. It was eighteen months since they'd split. It took him eight months before he slept with another woman and it was strange, not unpleasant, not earth shattering but like wearing new shoes. He slept with two other women in quick succession and knew he shouldn't compare them to Marilyn but couldn't help it. He resented this weakness in himself. She's not coming back, even if she did it would be a mistake so you're more the fool for protracting the inevitable, Karen is right, he thought, but she's wrong too. Marilyn and he were a conundrum, a circular square, yet he was still unable to move on with his life. As a boy he'd been fascinated by the story of Scott of the Antarctic who must have known he was pushing on to his doom. Clement had not meant it to act as a template for his behaviour but sometimes he felt it did.

The buzz of the flies drummed in his ears; the bored or weak ones who couldn't get to the blood were attracted to his sweat.

Clement made his way back to his vehicle through the same unwelcoming bush and the same over-friendly flies. They crawled up your nose and were in the back of your throat before you could blow them back out. En route he tried Graeme Earle. As expected the call went dead. Earle was the kind of bloke who loved this life, fishing, drinking, blue skies, wide open space and malevolent heat. You could never reach him on a rostered day off. Clement didn't rate him highly as a detective but to be fair, it wasn't like he was basing this on a great sample. They'd worked assaults, rapes and one tribal spat that turned into attempted murder. Earle's work was solid, he wasn't incompetent. It was more that, while this might be a massive region of thousands of ks, the crime garden was very small and there was nowhere to hone real detective skills so they stayed unborn or undeveloped. Earle had lived here fifteen years and in him Clement saw the traits more of a small town sheriff than a detective. He dialled Shepherd next. The detective constable answered his phone promptly.

'Guilty. Course the beak's given him a slap on the wrist. Three months.'

Shepherd couldn't finish a speech without some complaint.

On this occasion Clement sympathised. They'd gone after an inveterate wife-beater. Those cases were hard to get to court and when they got a sentence lighter than an empty cicada shell you felt you were in the wrong job on the wrong side of the planet. The women looked at you like you were the one who had given them the black eye or split lip.

Clement explained where he was and what he'd found, or rather hadn't. He told Shepherd they'd be setting up a crime scene.

'Bring Jared. And those guys who trapped the Callum Creek crocs. See if they're available.'

He opened his car and risked his bum on the scorching seat. He tapped the Pajero's plates into his computer. Bingo. Dieter Schaffer. DOB 14.04.48. As Jill had warned, the address was a lot number on Cape Leveque Road, a strip of bitumen that ran a hundred k north–south in a wilderness of mainly low scrub. The only phone number was the mobile he had. He did all this while Shepherd whinged about how hard it was going to be to do each of the tasks set. He ignored him.

'See you soon, Josh.'

Clement called the station and asked his desk sergeant, Mal Gross, if he knew a Dieter Schaffer. Of course he did. Gross knew most everybody in the Kimberley.

'Dieter. They call him "Schultz". Used to be a cop in Germany.'

So far as Gross was aware Schaffer lived alone in what was little more than a bush shack. Gross said he would get a car out there to look over the house but it was a good hundred k so Clement should not expect anything for a while.

Typical.

Clement fought his way back to the locus of his investigation. The missing outboard worried him but he began constructing plausible alternatives to murder-robbery. Dieter could have taken it with him in a mate's car. In fact he could have injured himself on it if the boat capsized. But while you could lose your phone in the accident, would you leave keys in the ignition? No, surely even if the battery had already run flat, you'd take the keys. Clement wondered if he should drive out and around to the yet-to-be-pegged crime scene but he was worried about driving over evidence so he was forced to yet again retrace his steps to the other side of the creek. Before leaving he took a swig of water, you could dehydrate fast out here. On the way the flies harassed him again. They bit him this time. He flicked them off as best he could.

Using the tent as the centre of the target, Clement began searching out in bands of about five metres deep. After around thirty minutes he found an area of flattened bush as if a vehicle had recently been there. He estimated it was about sixty metres north-west of the tent and would not have been visible from it. There was a bush track leading out from there, clearly used by vehicles for access. He'd always approached the creek from the eastern side, as the tourists had, but clearly there was some regular traffic came this way too. He followed the path for another hundred metres, calling out Schaffer's name but received no reply and doubled back. The bush was a level of incessant insect noise

Gradually he worked his way anticlockwise around the entire creek. There was the usual kind of litter: chocolate and chip wrappers, plastic bottles, beer cartons. He took photos of everything he encountered. The only piece of recent technology he gave credit to was the idea of a phone with a camera in it. So much easier than logging everything with a biro that wouldn't write on a cheap pad. Karen's comment needled him. It wasn't like he was trying to get back with Marilyn. Was he just terrified of another relationship, the unknown?

The dissolution of their relationship had caught him by surprise even though he supposed it had all the classic pointers.

They'd both let it go too far. It was like a DVD on your shelf you look over at every day, still in its case, telling yourself tonight was the night you'd watch it. But you never got around to it. There was always something more at hand, more demanding of you. Until she announces she's leaving and of course you say that's ridiculous and the fights start. Every grievance is dredged out. Pride flares. He offered to move out, the martyr. And before you know it, what was just bravado, a sympathy play, turns into the real thing and when you drag your sorry arse back and apologise it's too late. She's 'discovered' herself and how much you've 'inhibited' her.

Back to where he started, in more ways than one. His phone rang. Mal Gross. One of his mates had family near Dieter's shack. They'd driven over and taken a gander. Nobody was there. He had Di Rivi and Restoff heading there too but he thought the sooner Clement knew, the better. Clement thanked him and looked up to see a swirl of dust announce Shepherd's arrival. Jared Taylor, the aboriginal police aide, was with him, towing the trailer on which was mounted an inflatable boat. A tinny was lashed to the roof as back-up. Shepherd stepped out wearing the plastic white-framed sunnies Shane Warne had made famous in the late nineties. They looked ridiculous then and worse now. Shepherd was around one eighty-eight centimetres and fit, the build of a centre halfback, de rigeur tattoos just poking out from under short sleeves. Jared Taylor was shorter with a gut and, at forty, around twelve years older than Shepherd. Unlike Shepherd, he had a sunny disposition. They'd sparred in the ring once as part of Shepherd's training for the annual Kimberley v Gascoyne police comp. Naturally Shepherd fancied himself. Taylor's punches had nearly sent poor Shepherd through the ropes.

'What's the plan, Skip?'

Shepherd vocabulary reduced everything to a footy match.

'I guess we need to poke around for a body.'

Both of them looked at him, hoping he was joking. They didn't need to mention the croc. If it had overturned one tinny, why not another?

'Let's get to it.'

'Serious?'

'Yeah, Shep. Come on.'

'Shouldn't we wait for the croc blokes?'

'No time for that.'

They lifted the tinny off the roof of the vehicle and walked it to the water's edge keeping a wary eye. The creek was only shoulder-deep but too muddy to see into. Taylor had thought ahead and brought a couple of thin plastic rigid electrician's tubes, perfect as probes. He stayed on the bank, rifle ready, just in case. The little motor shattered the default static of bush noise. Clement guided the tinny to the far bank near Dieter's upturned tinny, cut the motor and they began probing the waters close to the shore. Gradually they worked their way out.

'Fucking flies,' grumbled Shepherd for the fiftieth time.

About twenty minutes in, Clement's pole struck something just below the surface, firmer than mud but too soft to be a rock or tree.

'Pass me the gaff.'

While he held the position, Shepherd passed over one of two gaff hooks. Clement sank it down, let it find purchase and pulled hard. The unmistakable shape of a body broke the surface.

(From *Waiting for the Cyclone*, a novel, forthcoming 2015.)

# PETER DOCKER

# NANA WAS RIGHT

**Somerset, outback Western Australia.**
Feel the heat. Feel its texture. Feel how the very air is woven into a denser pattern, with the stitches and purls falling back upon themselves. The heat blankets the country like a pea-soup fog, seeping right into the bones. Feel the heat radiate up from the land herself. The sun has gone now but it feels hotter still. The Old Man is a friend to the heat. The heat is like a cousin/brother he has known since birth. All the character nuances of the heat are as familiar as the smoke from the family fire. But not this heat. This hot wind is here at the wrong time. There has already been much discussion between the Old Man and his peers. What is the meaning of this heat at the wrong time? There is some great disturbance in atmospheres way beyond this continent—that is all that can be agreed upon. The Old Man knows that weather patterns here have their origins way to the north, around the mountain ranges of Pakistan and Afghanistan. The Old Man understands the connectivity of all things. Inside the heat, even this unseasonal heat, the only thing to be done is to survive. To go on living. Understanding will come later.

It's Anzac Day. 25th April. Ninety-odd years ago Australian and New Zealand soldiers under the control of English High Command swarmed onto the wrong beach in distant Turkey under a merciless hail of machine-gun and artillery fire. The Old Man knows the story of that first day only too well. His Grandfather told him the story over and over. It had been a warm day in Turkey as well. That story is woven into the family history, as well as the history of the nation to which his Grandfather did not officially belong. The truth is, his Grandfather never wanted to belong, and his exploits in the AIF had nothing to do with this thing that would later be thought of as a nation. Before Gallipoli and France, his Grandfather had little to do with white men and uniforms. And after, even less so. The Old Man knows exactly how his Grandfather felt. Things go in cycles—that is for sure.

Now the Old Man can see two white men in uniform. And him got no mob. All alone. They sit in the front of the brightly lit divvy van pulling up behind him. The Old Man turns off the engine of his Troopie. It is quiet now, with the police lights flashing across the deserted road, washing everything with momentary blue. The Old Man picks up the white can of Emu Export lager nestled between his legs, drains it, and drops the empty can on the floor of the passenger side with all the other shit. In his rear-view mirror, the Old Man sees Senior Constable Lishtokitz get out of the paddy wagon and start to come towards him. The Old Man sees the blast of heat hit the white man as he climbs out of the air-conditioned police vehicle. Lishtokitz almost staggers as though a bag of wheat was dropped onto his shoulders—but then catches himself and strides out to where the Old Man waits.

G'day mate, Lishtokitz says to the Old Man.

Hello, says the Old Man amiably.

Do you know why I've stopped you?

Cause I'm the only one drivin!

The Old Man cackles and looks around the deserted dirt track so that the younger white man can have a chance to get the joke. The younger man in uniform does not acknowledge the Old

Man's quip in any way. It's Anzac Day. Australians everywhere are drinking beer and burning meat while the Southern Cross and Union Jack against a background of blue flutters overhead. They are talking about far distant places like Gallipoli, Lae, Tobruk, Long Tan, and drinking more beer. They are playing two-up, discussing the colour of medal ribbons and their meanings, and drinking more beer.

This is a random breath test. I will require you to blow into the device with one long continuous blow.

Lishtokitz holds up the breathalyser to the Old Man. The Old Man regards the plastic tube suspiciously. He's been here before.

Have you been drinking, mate?

Only beer.

How many?

Eh?

How many *only beer*?

Yuwai. Only beer.

Fluent in five languages, English was the last one learnt, and the hardest for the Old Man. But even his grannies know that he understands more than he lets on. These are survival techniques on the frontier. The Old Man was living as a naked child of the desert, wild and free, when he was first studied by gudia anthropologists. They learned. He learned also.

One long continuous blow ...

The Old Man blows into the plastic tube. Senior Constable Lishtokitz steps back. He is sweating heavily now. The Old Man regards him evenly. Lishtokitz wants to watch the Old Man all the time. He's heard they can beat the breathalyser with their didgeridoo breathing techniques. But he can't hold the Old Man's eye. And isn't sure why. The hard ground beneath his feet feels soggy for a moment. The hand-held breathalyser beeps.

Sir, I am going to have to ask you to step out of the vehicle.

As soon as the *Sir* tumbles out of his mouth his mind juxtaposes it with *mate* like a Google-search. He went for Sir because you can't say *get out of the car, mate*. Now it all sounds wrong. It should have been Sir all along, the Google-search result seems to say. The Old Man doesn't move.

Get out of the car, now!

His voice is too loud in the desert night. The trees look on passively through the heat. Constable Slopken is getting out of the police vehicle and moving quickly to the scene, his right hand on his holstered Glock. The Old Man slowly opens the door of the Troopie. Not rushing is second nature to him. Rushing around can get you killed in the desert. You'd be walkin round dead. He climbs down and stands steadily in the desert night.

I'm placing you under arrest for DUI. Do you understand?

The Old Man smiles and holds out his hands ready to be cuffed.

Lishtokitz nods at Slopken who takes out his cuffs and places them on the Old Man's wrists. Slopken walks the Old Man back to the police vehicle. Lishtokitz leans in and takes the keys from the ignition of the Troopie. He winds up the driver's side window and locks the door. On the back seat Lishtokitz sees an old suit jacket with a little row of medals pinned to the lapel. For a moment he considers grabbing the Old Man's jacket—but fuck it, it's too hot. He goes back to the divvy van where Slopken is just climbing back in, having loaded the Old Man into the back. They drive in silence through Somerset back to the station, both men leaning forward to feel the cool air being blasted out by the aircon hitting their skin. It takes two minutes. The town could be a ghost town. The pub is full but the streets are empty. Somerset is named after some English lord, who no doubt never set foot in the place. He probably financed some prospectors, or graziers. These guys were like hedge fund managers investing in the joint venture of taking over WA. And they got to have things named after them as a bonus. That's the way these things go.

They pull up right out the front of the police station, and get the Old Man out of the back. They take him in through the heavy glass front doors. It's one of those low flat modern concrete buildings that looks like it is designed to withstand a cyclone, or a bomb attack.

Sergeant Smithers is standing at the front counter as they come in. The cop shop aircon is cold after the outside heat. The Old Man shivers as if someone just walked over his grave.

Well, look what the cat dragged in! calls Smithers.

Hello, says the Old Man as though nodding to a mate in the front bar.

Are you calling us cats, Sarge? asks Slopken.

DUI, says Lishtokitz to no one in particular.

Tjilpa, says the Old Man.

What's that? asks Smithers.

Tjilpa—desert cat, explains the Old Man.

We haven't dragged anyone, adds Slopken.

Wha'd ya cuff him for—ya Neanderthals? barks Smithers.

He held out his hands...

Get them off him. Get him processed. Fuck me dead.

Slopken takes off the handcuffs and they lead the Old Man through to the testing area. Smithers leans down to get some paperwork from under the counter.

What's up his arse? murmurs Slopken.

Smithers looks up.

It's Anzac Day, Slopken—something you wogs wouldn't understand.

Lishtokitz sits the Old Man down in the chair.

Whaddya mean, Sarge? Us New Aussies love the flag!

That flag has been draped on the coffins of our dead boys—ya can't wrap yourself in it and get pissed, or hang it out the back of your orange Commodore with mag wheels.

You having a go at my Commodore, Sarge?

You're outta your depth, Slopken.

One long continuous blow, says Lishtokitz, and holds the plastic tube out to the Old Man.

The Old Man blows into the device until it beeps, and then he sits back.

What's the reading? asks Smithers, already halfway through the form.

Zero point two three one.

What does that make it at time of offence?

Point two two two.

Slopken is looking over Smithers' shoulder as he does the form.

Do you know him? asks Slopken.

Course I fucken know him. He's a big boss man out at Burwarton.

Slopken doesn't know that Burwarton is another of the English peerage. He goes and gets the fingerprint station ready.

So he's the boss of a couple of tin sheds and a dozen car wrecks? comments Slopken with a twist of his mouth.

He laid the wreath this morning for the Aboriginal soldiers. That's why he's in town, says Smithers.

What's he a veteran of, the Battle of the Animal Bar?

He was in Vietnam, fuckhead. Recommended for the MC three times.

Did he ever get one?

Did Polly Farmer ever win a Brownlow?

I only follow European football, Sarge.

It's called soccer, you fucken dipshit!

Why do you go to the dawn service, Sarge? Anzac Day always puts you in a bad mood. You got medal envy?

Piss off!

Smithers is imagining Somerset and Burwarton getting together in a gentlemen's club in London for an Anzac Day drink. Sitting in fat leather armchairs toasting the Queen with forty-year-old Scotch, patting themselves on the back for providing the Empire with such robust and ready cannon fodder. Smithers shakes off the fantasy and steps up to the Old Man. The Old Man sits quietly with his eyes closed.

You are under arrest for driving under the influence, with a blood alcohol reading of point two two two. Do you understand?

The Old Man nods.

You will also be charged with driving contrary to conditions of an extraordinary licence. Do you understand?

The Old Man nods again.

Now, I'm gonna haveta send you to Baal in the morning. Do you understand?

The Old Man nods. His gaze seems to fall on nothing in the police station. He is thinking of a song. Feeling for it. He's not sure what it is yet. It's this place.

Because you're a cheeky fella. Cheeky fulla go walkabout. You walkabout—no show court.

The Old Man smiles as if at a memory.

I wanna go to sleep, he says.

His eyes are closed as if he is finished with this procedure now, and doesn't want to look on these images. The world we can see is an illusion. He closes his eyes as if he is imagining himself away from this place. Out in his beloved desert country. Away from white man police. Away from Anzac Day and all the talk of sacrifice.

You want me to ring someone in Burwarton?

Sleep now, the Old Man says to the polished concrete floor.

All right. You sleep. Tomorrow Baal lockup.

Slopken ushers the Old Man over to the processing area. At

10:10 pm Smithers signs the Form 5 bail record form, refusing the prisoner bail.

It was only last year when Smithers attended court as a witness in a case against the Old Man, and the Old Man didn't show. Going to court is such a pain in the arse. A day lost.

Smithers records two reasons: if the accused is not kept in custody he/she may fail to appear in court in accordance with his bail undertaking; and if the accused is not kept in custody, he/she may commit an offence. At 10:15 pm Smithers picks up the phone and dials. It rings for a long time. A woman answers.

Rankin.

Sergeant Smithers, Somerset Police.

Yeah.

I have a prisoner for transport tomorrow morning.

You're kidding.

I'm not.

It's Sunday on a long weekend.

What's your point?

Bail him and he can appear in your court next Tuesday.

We'll bail him and he'll go walkabout. I want you to pick him up tomorrow morning.

Rightio then.

As long as it's not too much trouble.

Get fucked.

She hangs up. Smithers puts down the receiver, shakes his head. The worst thing the state ever did was to privatise the prisoner transport. It's always the same with the GPL4 supervisor, Rankin. Wouldn't work in an iron lung. Smithers looks over and nods to Slopken.

Slopken leads the prisoner out to the cells area. It's empty. All the mob are out at the community where the Old Man has driven in from. No one in town to fill the cells tonight. No animals for the Animal Bar. That's why the cops are driving around bored. Don't know how to do nothin—these fullas. The Old Man goes into the cell and is lying on the bench by the time the open-barred door clangs shut behind him. Slopken doesn't mean to slam the door, but it's so heavy that even a little bit of momentum in the door-swing will guarantee a cage-shaking locking of the cell. 10.30 pm. Anzac Day.

When the Old Man wakes he is dehydrated and disorientated. There are two white men standing at the cell door talking: a policeman, and the local JP, Finn Macomish. Macomish is a red-faced stocky bloke. He holds his akubra hat in his hands, and constantly smooths down the front brim. The Old Man recognises the cop.

Charleston, says the Old Man, and moves his feet in a one-two shuffle gesture, originating in his knees, to demonstrate the charleston.

Senior Constable Charleston smiles.

Hello, Old Man.

Him your good boy? the Old Man asks, so fast and running all the words together, that Macomish the JP misses it. He is looking at the brim of his hat.

You have to get used to the desert accent. Charleston smiles and nods. The JP has lived out here all his life, and still can barely understand a word.

The Old Man grins to himself.

Good morning, says the good boy. Had a few drinks last night, did we?

The JP speaks too slowly and too loudly, like an Australian tourist ordering soup in Saigon. Charleston rolls his eyes. He knows this is just Smithers' usual bullshit but there is nothing he can do about it. The Old Man should've been released on bail.

Water? asks the Old Man.

The JP asks him his name. He tells them his white man name,

cause that's what they want to hear. The JP tells him that he's gotta go to Baal. Already knew that. The policeman sends his good boy away.

You got im cuppatea?

Charleston smiles, unlocks the cell, and leads the Old Man out the back of the station to the kitchen area.

Ngamari?

Charleston nods and takes out his Winnie Blues and gives the Old Man two cigarettes. The Old Man looks at the two tailor-mades in his hand.

Waru?

Charleston hands over his lighter.

Kettle, tea, sugar—help yourself. You can go out the back, he says, and gestures to the backyard.

The Old Man makes himself a cuppatea. He uses two teabags, four sugars and a generous splash of long-life milk—all in the big fat CIB mug. Then he carries the big fat CIB mug out the back door of the station. He finds a spot near the cyclone fence where he can sit on an old drum. He sits down, places his mug of tea on the red earth, takes out the first cigarette, and lights it up. He takes a draw on the smoke and looks up. Just above is a big old wurrung, his black feathers iridescent in the morning sunshine. Their eyes meet and they let out a little sigh. The crow flies off. The Old Man applies himself to his cigarette.

Charleston is at the front counter when the GPL4 Mazda van pulls up.

What a heap of shit, thinks Charleston.

Howell comes in first, with Stockbow just behind him. Howell looks like he doesn't belong in uniform, even the shitty grey GPL4 attire. There is a knack to wearing a uniform. And you've gotta have pride. To Howell the uniform is just clothes. He has heavy rings around his eyes, and his skin is puffy and red. His gut hangs over his belt. Charleston was born in his police uniform.

He works hard in Lishtokitz's backyard gym, and he hates fat people. Greedy and lazy. They walk in mid-argument.

Well ya shouldn't have fucken said yes if ya didn't wanna come, Howell says.

Don't be a wanker, I'm just sayin ... says Stockbow.

She stops when she sees Charleston. Charleston is why she really came.

Senior Constable Charleston, she says, and tries to look bright.

Youse both look like shit, comments Charleston.

Smithers' bullshit is really starting to grate now that these clowns are here.

Anzac Day. Didn't ya have a sip? asks Stockbow hopefully.

Dawn service. Then I went for a long run, says Charleston.

It was too hot.

I love the heat, says Charleston flatly.

Me too, says Stockbow, but not this time of year. Felt like Australia Day. Fucking climate change.

It's all Greek to me, says Charleston.

We're here for prisoner transport, says Howell.

Charleston flicks a pile of papers onto the counter between them.

Sign here, here, and here.

Howell checks the entries.

When ya comin to Baal next? asks Stockbow.

I'll get your passenger.

Charleston goes back to the cell. The door is wide open and it is empty.

He heads out to the kitchen area.

Uncle?

The Old Man is outside having his last cigarette. He finishes it and stubs the butt out in the red dust. He slowly gets to his feet and shuffles towards the door. He doesn't want to go. But he knows full well that this is what the whitefullas do—they love to move people around, especially if it is off-country. Charleston grabs the only water bottle from the fridge.

I got this, the Old Man says, and shows Charleston the frozen pie he took out of the freezer.

Charleston smiles and nods.

You right, he says.

When they emerge from the cells area, Howell and Stockbow are outside by the van. Charleston looks at her through the heavy glass doors. She should be attractive—but why isn't she? Women are certainly hard to come by out here. Charleston leads the Old Man through the doors.

You got water? asks Charleston.

In the front, says Howell.

For the Old Man, reiterates Charleston, as though talking to children.

Howell and Stockbow look at each other.

I got this, but it's only six hundred mil, Charleston says, and hands the bottle to the Old Man.

Howell gets the back doors of the Mazda open. The Old Man looks in doubtfully. All four of them can feel the heat radiating out from the cell pod.

The sooner you get in, the sooner the aircon kicks in, offers Stockbow.

Charleston gives her a look. He's gonna give Smithers a serve when he sees him.

Is it working?

Course it works. Ya gotta get in, mate. Then it comes on.

Charleston glares at her.

Why didn't you put it on before to cool it down?

Stockbow ignores Charleston and concentrates on the Old Man.

The sooner you get in, the sooner it comes on, she repeats.

Howell moves closer to the Old Man.

Carn, mate, in ya get.

The Old Man turns to Charleston. Charleston can't meet his gaze and turns away. The Old Man gingerly climbs into the prisoner pod like he's picking his way across sharp hot rocks. Howell quickly locks and bolts the inner and outer door.

Thanks, mate, Howell says to Charleston, and gets in the driver's side.

Stockbow looks across to Charleston who is wishing the earth would swallow him up. She takes a step in.

Call me, Steve, she says.

OK. You're Steve.

C'mon, Steve.

See ya, he says through a tight jaw.

She turns and climbs into the Mazda van. They take off. A small article of blue rubbish is blown across the police driveway, and the van drives right over it. Charleston takes a few steps to pick the rubbish up. He bends and grabs it, only to realise that it is one of the little Australian flags made in China that would've been adorning a lairy ute only a few hours before on the national remembrance day. Charleston stands there for a moment holding the crumpled little blue nylon flag, watching the white van go. Warming up a bit. Good one. He turns and goes back into the police station, dropping the blue rubbish into the small plastic bin near the counter.

In the back of the van, the Old Man already knows that he's made a terrible mistake. He should've refused to get in. Should've appealed to Charleston. It's too hot.

*There is no fucken aircon.*

The seats are metal benches, already too hot to sit on. There are no handles to hold onto to stand up. And Baal is nearly four hours away. He puts down the pie and the water bottle. It's too hot. This heat is the wrong kind. All this steel.

It's an oven. The gudia will cook him. His nana was right. White men will steal you in the night, then cook you and eat you.

He stands with his feet apart, jammed against the benches at the base.

There is one small window up high, but he can't see out of it. Not being able to see the country is a torture in itself. The Old Man loves to drive through the country, and when the road comes close to a songline, which it does in several places, he can look out the window and read/feel the Tjukurrpa as he goes, even singing out the story. But now there is nothing. No chance for anything but to get hotter and hotter. He bangs on the hot steel of the wall that is closest to the driving compartment. He pounds out a storm. A battle rages in his fists against the blistering steel. The sweat pours off him. He knows this exertion is wrong. But he is trapped now. His fists eventually die down to a slow song, and then silence. He listens. Nothing. Just the humming rattling roar of the old Mazda engine, dragging them relentlessly down the baking tarmac. He takes off his shirt, his fingers fumbling with the buttons. The heat seeps into him, sears its way in like slow-motion lightning. He remembers finding the sand melted into glass tubes by lightning as a child in the desert. How fragile they were. He drops his shirt to the floor. His head is buzzing like the burning road snaking away beneath the moving cell. He tries stamping his feet. There is no give in the metal floor. He sits on the bench and kicks at the inner door. It is solid and the hot metal bench scorches him through his jeans. He jumps up. He starts to sing a song low in his throat; a single phrase in his Nana's tongue repeated over and over. Calling out to Country. He sees the water bottle and goes to bend forward to grab it. The van suddenly lurches sideways; he loses his balance and goes down hard, smashing his left eye into the edge of the metal bench. He lies on the metal floor between the facing metal benches, blood pouring from the deep cut over his left eye. The pouring blood obscures the sight in his left eye and his right vision is blurry. The song tumbles soundlessly out of his lips as his core temperature skyrockets, and his internal organs begin to collapse one by one.

Until only the Old Man's heart and his voiceless song throb through the crushing heat. Eventually his heart begins to slow, the compartment is filled with the stench of human flesh cooking, and the song is released.

Stockbow doesn't wake until one of her iPod earphones has fallen from her left ear. Howell drives. The road snakes away in front of them to the shimmering horizon.

How long have I been asleep?

Hours.

Prisoner settle down?

Stopped banging ages ago.

Didn't have much rhythm.

They count different.

Stockbow drinks from her water bottle. The engine rattles away beneath them. Howell leans forward, resting with his elbows on the steering wheel.

You want me to drive?

I'm not fucken stoppin.

They drive in silence. Stockbow leans over and taps the small CCTV screen on the dash. Nothing. She puts her left earphone back in and selects a track. Jimmy Barnes: 'Driving Wheels'. She slumps back against her closed window and stares out at the passing low scrub and red dust country. She doesn't really go to sleep but doesn't really stay awake. The country hypnotises her with its sameness, with its bigness, with its unknowability. Her hangover vibrates with the drums and bass on 'Driving Wheels'. She vagues right out.

Eventually Howell's voice cuts in.

You wanna ring the prison?

Are we that close?

Look around.

Stockbow leans over and taps the CCTV screen. It flickers then stops, for a moment a perfect black-and-white image of the prisoner pod. The Old Man is facedown. The screen flickers again.

We should check on him.

I'm not stoppin.

He's facedown with his shirt off.

Howell's lips go tight and he slows the van.

Just get him to put his shirt on and drink some fucken water!

The van pulls over, raising a little red dust cloud on the shoulder of the highway. They are getting close to the big sheds and big yards stuffed with big machinery that is the industrial area on the outskirts of Baal. The GPL4 officers climb out. Stockbow takes the keys and Howell stretches. She gets the outer doors open. The metal is hot to touch. She can see the Old Man is shirtless and facedown. She can see the pool of blood from his bleeding face.

We gotta get him out.

Howell arrives at the back of the vehicle.

We can't open the inner door, he says.

He's bloody hot.

They live in the fucken desert.

HEY! OLD MAN! HEY!

There is no response from the Old Man.

He might be dead, Stockbow says quietly.

He's not fucken dead. They live in the desert.

Let's open up.

I'm ringing Rankin.

He pulls out his phone and dials.

Rankin.

Yeah, it's me. We got a problem.

Broken down again?

It's the prisoner. Passed out.

What's wrong?

He's hung-over and didn't drink his water. Took his shirt off.

Turn the aircon up.

The aircon doesn't fucken work.

Since when?

Oh, for fuck's sake.

Get his shirt on. Take him to prison.

We can't deliver him unconscious.

Take him to the hospital. I'll meet you there.

The phone goes dead. Howell rings again. Nothing.

What? Stockbow demands.

Fucken reception.

Wha'd she say?

Get his shirt on, get him to drink, get him to hospital.

He's not gonna drink. He's out to it.

He's just hung-over. Get his shirt on.

You're hung-over.

So're you. Get his shirt on.

I'm not touching him.

It looks like we knew he was hot and did nothing!

How could we know?

The aircon's not even fucken working!

Everyone knows that.

Not him! Howell says, jerking an angry thumb at the prone figure.

He fucken does now!

Just get his shirt on.

They open the inner door and the heat and the stench of burning flesh blasts out at them.

Fuck, she says under her breath, and climbs in.

The heat is overwhelming and Stockbow breaks out in an instant all-over sweat. She rolls the Old Man over and sees the burn on his guts.

Shit.

Howell sees it too. It is serious—a deep burn taking up half his abdomen raised up and angry red and orange, in the shape of the rising sun badge of the ADF, complete with sun rays coming out of the crown where the burning flesh of the Old Man must've had little folds where he fell. Neither of the GPL4 officers recognise the shape.

Just get the shirt on him, urges Howell.

I think he's dead.

He's not dead. Get on with it.

But the Old Man is too heavy. She gets the sleeves over each wrist.

You pull him forward.

Howell half climbs in and gets the Old Man around the shoulders and pulls him forward. The cut over his eye looks deep. Stockbow slides the shirt up his arms and down over his front. Howell eases the torso back down and the Old Man's head hits the hot metal floor with a clunk. She quickly gets the buttons done back up and gets out. Howell is on the doors immediately, shooting the bolts and locking them. She stands by the road panting and sweating heavily. Howell's shirt is so wet from sweat that he looks like someone has poured a bucket of water over him. Stockbow gathers herself, and they head for the cabin.

Hurry up. He might die.

He won't die.

He might already be dead. I couldn't feel no pulse.

Howell starts the engine. It coughs and splutters. He slams it into gear and they head for the hospital. All around them are massive red slag heaps baking in the sun, as though the town of Baalboorlie is ringed with the shallow graves of giants.

(From *Sweet One*, a novel, 2014.)

# JULIENNE VAN LOON

## HE LOST HER TWICE

This sort of heat was too much for somebody his age. It was only nine in the morning, and already so ruthlessly bright. Back home in Thailand, the rainy season had only just finished and the moist air felt close and warm. This dry Australian air was different. He felt exposed by it.

Rattuwat turned back towards the bushland path they'd left half an hour before. At least there was some shade in that direction. It was unwise, actually, to have ever left the vehicle. But the child had convinced him that they were already very close to the prison and so he had begun walking for her sake. She was a child, after all, and she deserved to be able to see her father, especially after everything that had happened. Ah, Rattuwat, he thought to himself, you have been a fool to believe an eight year old's view of the world.

And now what? What could he do? The child had no respect. The child was impatient and rude. She did not understand that an old man like himself could not walk this sort of distance, especially in such heat. He took another step towards the shade of the trees, but paused to glance back over his shoulder at the girl. She was now just two twigs for legs sticking out beneath a faded red dress. She was a small girl in a big landscape. And was it wise, he wondered, to leave this girl on her own, to turn away from her out here in a place like this? What if she were your own daughter, he thought, and he remembered Sua at a similar age, so many years ago, the way she would skip in circles around him in the family's electrical appliances shop in Ubon Ratchathani, her skirt flapping, her grin wide. Rattuwat touched his hand at his chest again. The burning pain was back. He stood motionless in the bare paddock. The sun beat down and he was overcome with grief. The little red dress walked on. 'She not know where to go,' he said, though nobody could hear him.

That little baby girl of his—the one who was dead now—he still remembered precisely how small she was when she was born, the length of her no greater than his own forearm. She came nearly two weeks later than predicted, and she did so back-to-front, causing her mother a long and painful labour. When Rattuwat held his daughter for the first time he pulled aside the soft white muslin wrap and retrieved her hand. She wrapped her fingers around one of his as he looked closely into her red and angry face. Rattuwat had come to parenting at a mature age, already into his fifties, but when he looked at that baby's face he felt a sense of awe that he had never felt before. It seemed the girl knew already something of what life was about. And while she had put up what resistance she could during the labour, it was the only tantrum she ever had. Rattuwat gave her the nick-name Juum, meaning splash, because she had arrived so dramatically, but thereafter settled quickly into peacefulness. Within weeks she was sleeping and feeding in a predictable pattern that came to foreshadow her placid and good-natured approach to everyday life. She rarely cried.

Their neighbourhood in Ubon Ratchathani marvelled for years about the time when Sua was three years old, and she was trampled by an angry buffalo, leaving her with fierce bruising and a broken wrist. Afterwards, she simply picked herself up from the ground and wiped the dirt from her hands. '*Pôr*,' she said, looking up at her father, 'I hurt me.' There were no tears.

Rattuwat and Thawin had kept every letter, every postcard their adult daughter had sent to them from Australia. The collection was piled into a small cardboard box in their single room in the modern-style multistorey building they had moved into after the children had left. And though he was now struggling to find any truth at all in the quaint domestic narrative his daughter had wanted him and her mother to believe, he still felt nervous to think of that little bundle of papers, so far away. He was itching to read them all over again, to look for clues between the lines. His daughter's handwriting was neat and careful, the paper lightweight and pale blue, the kind reserved for airmail. It was all they had left of her now.

Perhaps, for all his doting, he had not been the most careful of fathers.

In 1997, they were still living above the family whitegoods business in Ubon Ratchathani. If not for the financial crisis of the late nineties, they might still be there now, his brother, their two wives, the children and grandchildren. It was a dream Rattuwat indulged in occasionally. In fact, he knew that if had he not left the bulk of the financial decisions to his brother in the first place, they might have got through even that period. Proi was a risk-taker. That was always clear. But the scale of his risk-taking went unnoticed for too many years. When the stock market floundered in the capital, Rattuwat made the trip to Bangkok to try to ensure supply of their stock from a trader whose father had once been a close friend of their own father. When he got there, he discovered the truth: the entire value of the business had been fully mortgaged for some years, and the stocks Proi had gambled on were worthless. Their company was 1.3 million baht in debt. But that was not the worst of it. Within days of Rattuwat's discovery, Proi was dead.

When Rattuwat got home to Ubon, already burdened with the news of his brother's suicide, he witnessed a more confounding sense of loss on the face of his own wife.

'Juum has disappeared,' she told him.

'What do you mean? How could she have disappeared?'

'Two days ago. She helped me prepare the first meal, she never came to the second.'

'How could she disappear between the house and the school? There is only a few blocks to walk. Everybody knows her there. Where did you look?'

'I have looked. Everybody has looked. She is nowhere.'

For Rattuwat and his wife, those three years between 1997 and 2000 were the longest years of their married life. Bankrupt and heartbroken, they moved back to Warin Chamrap, the village in which Rattuwat's parents were born, and lived with his peasant cousins, fourteen family members in a one-room house. Daily life was reduced to a dull and exhausting pattern of physical labour in the fields. Rattuwat and Thawin withdrew from each other and from their sons, Arthit and Lek, each carrying out their daily work with a solemnity that was new to their once lighthearted family. Juum's name was barely spoken between them: they struggled just to carry on, to save face. Rattuwat went more regularly to the nearby forest monastery to speak to the head monk, who gave him the same simple advice about the eight winds, the eight conditions and the value of non-attachment he had been giving him all his life. In the third year, at the Bun Bang Fai festival, Rattuwat and Thawin got drunk together and broke their silence about their daughter. They talked for a long time about everything that had happened, and they decided to release a bird for Juum; it was a traditional gesture, aimed at setting her spirit free. Even if it would not bring Sua back, perhaps it would help to cure their unhappiness, or to lighten the impact of their poverty. They arranged it with the bird handler, and Rattuwat felt a weight shift from his shoulders as soon as the white bird fled its cage. A glance across at Thawin and he knew that she felt the same.

The following afternoon, a teenager in blue jeans, carrying a small handbag, stepped off the *songthaew* from Ubon. It was Sua.

The girl who stepped back into Rattuwat's family that May was different to the one they'd known three years earlier. Her body had become the body of a young woman, and she was beautiful, despite the awful Western-style clothes. But it was her face that struck them as so different. Her expression revealed immediately to Rattuwat that she had seen too much. She held her head up high all the way along the dirt lane to her paternal grandmother's house, but when she knelt in front of her parents on the old grass mat upstairs, she burst into tears.

It took years to find out the truth about what had happened. If Rattuwat had been given access to the facts in 1997 he could probably have saved Sua from those years. He could have tracked her down, somehow, bargained her back. But the cruelty was this: of all the rumours that reached his family's ears during that time in the old village, none of them steered anywhere near the truth. The day before he died, Rattuwat's brother had traded his niece to people traffickers to settle a personal debt. As it turned out, everybody in their old district knew, but nobody had the courage to mention it directly to Rattuwat and his wife.

They lost her again in 2005, not long after Rattuwat found himself sitting across from the big Australian man—Steve—at the makeshift tables beside their local noodle seller in Bangkok. Steve was not well dressed. His singlet, with great armholes, showed half his torso, and his baggy shorts, a faded khaki green, had a large ink stain on the left pocket. He wore flip-flops. Was this any way to dress to meet your potential father-in-law?

'She is a good daughter,' he said to the Australian. '*Lôok saao dee.*'

'Don't worry, mate,' said Steve. 'I look after girl.' He grinned broadly and nodded, pointing to himself and then at Sua. 'I look after girl.'

Rattuwat looked away, embarrassed.

This was not what he and Thawin had in mind for their only daughter. The family had been living in Bangkok almost a full year, and Sua had a good job at the cosmetics counter at the big retailer MBK. She was happy there. Nobody here knew anything about the stolen years. The twins, too, were happy in their new roles with the local *motorcy* gang, ferrying the local commuters up and down the *soi*, every day a game of strategy and chance, a kind of sport. But now, here was the Australian man, eager to split the five of them up.

Rattuwat watched sweat forming on Steve Manning's brow and thought it unlikely that any good would come of the marriage. Most of the men in their neighbourhood would consider it a blessing to have a daughter good-looking enough to draw the attentions of a rich farang, to have one of the family put down roots in a Western country like Australia, but Rattuwat watched the Australian carefully across the table and could see no reason to rejoice.

And yet it was what she wanted, the girl. It was all she talked about. Rattuwat could not bring himself to disappoint her.

When the day came to leave for the airport, Thawin could not bear to go to wave them off. She did not even want to witness Sua packing her clothes into the small black suitcase-on-wheels which the Australian had given her. She sat on their shared bed watching the television.

Rattuwat and the boys rode with Sua and the Australian to Don Muang Airport in the metered taxi. While they waited in the traffic on the Vibhavadi Road, Rattuwat took off one of several amulets that hung around his neck and held it forth in both hands, nodding at his daughter.

'This was my grandmother's,' he said.

Sua took the amulet in both hands while her brothers looked on. It was a tiny buddha carved in tiger tooth, mounted inside a small silver and glass case. It was the most valuable thing their family now owned.

'For protection.'

'*Pôr*, this is yours,' she said, 'you need it for yourself.'

'Take it. You don't know what can happen in a foreign country. You are still young, Juum. You need plenty of luck.'

Rattuwat looked his daughter in the eye. He found himself unable to interpret her expression. Was she sad or happy? Was she sure about what she was doing? This was to be the last time he would ever see her alive, and a part of him sensed it, even then.

'You are a good daughter,' he said to her. 'A good daughter.'

After Sua left, Rattuwat sometimes allowed himself to imagine that her marriage to the farang would mean a move to Australia for himself and Thawin; that they might live out their old age in their son-in-law's first-world house, Sua tending to them in their frailty, they, in turn, lending their wisdom to the grandchildren. His Isaan friends, living in Bangkok, encouraged this fantasy, indeed they believed it the chief reason for seeking out such a marriage for any eligible daughter. It was perhaps this foolish but persistent daydream that had allowed him and his wife to loosen up on the supervision of their sons, to fail to pay the right sort of attention when the boys became distant and moody. Rattuwat could not put his finger on the precise day or week or month he lost his boys to the slum gang. If he had been aware of it, he might have moved more swiftly to prevent the situation. If he had been aware of it, he would never have let them go.

'The door to my house is always open to you,' he had often promised his children. And it was true: the door was open. But the children chose to walk through it less and less.

When he took the urgent phonecall from the Australian—the second Australian, Dave—and registered the news of his daughter's death, Rattuwat walked away from his post at Park Plaza Sukhumvit and went immediately in search of the twins at the headquarters of the outlaw *motorcy* gang buried deep in the slums of Kloeng Toey. It was a risk even to walk those narrow dirt streets in that neighbourhood, and he was threatened by several gatekeepers, and by a volley of dogs, but he needed the boys to know, and further, for them to be with him when he broke the news to their mother. When Arthit and Lek finally appeared in the doorway of a makeshift hovel, Rattuwat could see from the look in their eyes that they were no longer completely human. The boys were twin ghosts. There was barely the slightest recognition at the name of their sister; the word death meant even less to them. They refused to come home.

From his position beneath the ancient Australian tree, surveying the dry, salt-pocked farming land, Rattuwat tasted only regret. He should have done more to fight for his children, all of them. He supposed he had trusted them to find their own way, make their own mistakes. He had never sought to control them in the manner of his own father. Now he wondered whether that approach was a poor excuse for laziness. In his mind, he heard again the distant voice of Vithi, son of the politician for whom Rattuwat had worked as a driver in Bangkok during his youth.

'You people from Isaan, you are put to work like dogs,' Vithi said to Rattuwat once, catching his eye in the rear-view mirror as he sat on the softly upholstered leather seat of his father's luxury car. 'Listen comrade, you see the slums here in Bangkok, they are full of farming people. Our people, Thai people, are starving right here in the capital, while the ruling class get fat on English teacake, looking ridiculous in those cheap Western suits.'

Rattuwat didn't always know how to respond to Vithi. He did not want to cause any trouble. Most of the time he said nothing.

'You see? You see how you are?' the university student would chide him. 'How can you improve your people's lot when you are so passive? This is the problem with our country. Somebody shits in our cooking pot, right in the middle of our house, and all we can do is kneel down and *wai* to them in gratitude.'

Once, Rattuwat quoted the Buddha to him: 'Holding on to anger is like grasping a hot coal.'

Vithi scoffed. 'It is so convenient isn't it? Have you ever thought about that? The Dharma tells us not to get angry, no matter what the ruling dictators choose to do to us. In this fashion, we are docile. We are too easy to manipulate. No, we are fools.'

Remembering this now, Rattuwat shook his head. Poor Vithi. He was the first real communist Rattuwat had ever met. And he was long dead now: shot dead by Field Marshal Sarit's men in 1963. Four decades had passed and the young man's voice still followed his one-time chauffeur around.

Actually, right now, Rattuwat was almost as destitute as he had been in the fifties, in the days before he took the job driving for Vithi's father. Two days ago, he had changed his last two thousand baht at the airport in Bangkok. It amounted to fifty Australian dollars. Half of this he had spent yesterday at the little supermarket near his son-in-law's house. He had bought flowers for the makeshift altar to his daughter that he had set up in the main room of the cottage, and then he had bought food for himself and the little girl. Now, he had a little less than twenty Australian dollars in his pocket. If he could not find his way back to the car, to the girl, to the little house in the paddock in which his daughter had spent her last years, he might even die here himself.

For the first time since the dim days of the nineteen seventies—six years he spent in a prison camp by the Mekong River—Rattuwat felt almost completely bereft of hope. He longed for the company of his wife, the touch of her nose against his. He looked up at the sun and envied its relentless strength. I have failed each and every one of my children, he thought. And then he gazed across the dry paddock and noticed a farm tractor, edging the perimeter. So, there was life here, after all. He stood, as carefully as he could, and waved his arms in the direction of the farmer.

'Hello?' he called. 'Hello!'

But he might as well have been made from glass. The tractor turned the corner of the paddock and receded into the distance.

(From *Harmless*, a novella, 2013.)

# ADAM MORRIS

## REUNION

He had been kidding himself. Professional musician. He would bandy the term around to convince himself as well as others. He wondered if Zappa had ever had to mark assignments on what fourteen year old illiterates think of Grecian urns. Was Bono ever a teacher at Mountjoy Prison? Professional musician my balls. It wasn't until his meeting with an old schoolfriend that Saul truly realised what a stretch it had been. He was sitting drinking with Pat, who Saul had run into at one of his gigs. Saul was on stage in a small pub playing with a bass player on his right and a mandolin player on his left. The gig was going all right; the place was half full, about a dozen people up dancing. And out of the corner of his eye Saul saw Pat sitting at the bar. He looked well; he had lost quite a bit of weight since high school. Saul was glad to see him, glad to see him from the stage; he was glad his old friend was seeing him in such good form too, on stage, a professional musician.

After the set was over he headed over to say hello. Pat gave him a smile, he looked happy, genuinely happy. He told Saul he looked the same as he did when they were in school. Saul repaid the compliment but added a mention about Pat's weight loss. Mentioning weight loss was always difficult for Saul, especially with women. He basically felt like he was saying you're not such a fat cunt anymore. He generally avoided it with women altogether. Pat was drinking vodka. Vodka and lime. The last time Saul had seen him was the year after high school and Pat wouldn't go near anything but beer or those horrible creamed liqueurs. Those drinks that bastards poured down teenage girls' throats with the intention of raping them when they pass out. Nasty stuff. At least Pat wasn't drinking that now. Maybe that was the key to his weight loss. Saul would learn over the course of the evening that Pat had many strategies in place to keep the wolf of his weight at bay.

Over the next twenty minutes Saul and Pat chatted in that way old friends who haven't seen each other in years do. Subtly dropping in evidence of achievement without clearly declaring anything outright that suggested they'd turned into a self-obsessed egomaniac. 'Turned into' was the phrase that made Saul laugh. Pat was working as a fashion photographer in much the same way as Saul was working as a musician. Pat also worked on the side. One of his regular jobs was for a community paper taking pictures of new shop owners or business initiatives, such as a new local dog wash outside the vet clinic or the fundraising efforts of a couple of eleven year old girls who raised enough money selling homemade scrunchies to buy an elderly neighbour (who was recently broken into, who Pat also photographed a few weeks before) a motion sensitive spotlight for her front porch. And once a week Pat would teach a beginners course in photography at a local TAFE college. He worked with a camera for a living the way Saul worked with his guitar. Sometimes he used his camera to take photos, sometimes those photos ended up on billboards and glossy magazines, sometimes they ended up in a community paper advertising a steak night for a local tavern and sometimes he just took it out of its box and showed people how to turn it on. Professional photographer. Saul had to head back on stage for the last set. Pat said he'd stick around and they could have a drink after and catch up some more.

Saul finished up the last set; it was a pretty good one, the bass player had gotten himself drunk, but not spastic drunk and the mandolin player was always brilliant no matter what state he was in. Saul was fairly drunk himself and enjoyed the end of the gig. He packed away, got paid from the manager and paid the other two musicians. The last set they had played for longer than they were supposed to, the pack-up had taken awhile, and by the time everything was in order the pub had called last drinks, the lights were getting turned on and the bar staff were cleaning down the place in a hurry to get home. So instead of staying they decided to go back to Pat's house.

Pat lived in a shithole. This immediately made Saul feel better about himself. He realised the fault in this way of thinking, but enjoyed it anyway. They walked through the front door and it looked like someone had robbed the place. Saul didn't say anything, he was half-expecting Pat to start jumping up and down and calling for the cops. Pat just kept on walking, threw his keys down on a hallway table that had ashtrays, cups, magazines, an old shirt and what looked like half a chessboard. No robbery, no cops. There were boxes in the hallway like somebody was moving in, or out. Keyboards, an electric guitar, a set of hand weights, photography magazines and hardcover books. Old, old carpets, brown running from wall to wall into yellowed stained bedsheets that hung from the walls as curtains. They moved on down the hallway passing two bedrooms as they went. Ratty single beds, like teenagers' rooms, one after the other. Maybe Pat had kids. Maybe these were their bedrooms and they had just taken over the house. The lounge room was no different, ashtrays everywhere, film posters stuck with blutack on the wall, an old TV with wooden panelling, a PlayStation on the ground littered with a few games, even a milk crate with a candle in a saucer sitting on top of it. If this wasn't Pat's real house, he had created one hell of an installation.

They were heading for the kitchen. That's where Pat did his entertaining. It was like an old Tom and Jerry cartoon: plates and pots and pans nearly to the ceiling, empty jars, open cans of food, rubbish bin overflowing. This was worse than Ralph's shed. Pat was living in squalor. And apart from the other bedrooms it looked like he was living alone. It was hard to assign ownership to rubbish. Was all this shit possibly Pat's? Was this how he really lived? How could he bring people back to this? They finally made it to the table, Pat poured some cheap wine. After those months in Ralph's shed, Saul felt fairly comfortable.

They talked about how Saul never played music at high school, just like Pat never took photos. They asked each other about their brothers and sisters and about their parents. They had had sleepovers as teenagers at each other's houses, they went on camp together and now here they both were, drinking only the wine they could afford.

By all accounts Pat should be as miserable as Saul but there was a difference that Saul noticed with Pat. Although neither had bought a house, got married or had children and neither had really anything to show for himself, Pat did have that smile. It wasn't as powerfully joyful as the minister's, but it was definitely there. He had a lightness about him. He didn't seem to mind the squalor. And the way he talked suggested that he didn't seem to worry the way Saul worried. He didn't seem to think about things the way Saul found himself thinking about things. Saul couldn't imagine Pat filling out a negative thought diary. In his face was evidence of that happiness that Saul had never seen in his own life, at any stage of his life.

Saul and Pat ended up drinking into the night. Saul fell asleep on the couch. By all accounts it had been a good night.

Saul woke early the next morning and headed out without waking Pat. The early morning with little sleep and two or three bottles of red wine the night before made the worst hangovers for Saul. Beer had nearly no effect on him at all the next day. A night of whisky drinking left him feeling stoned until the next afternoon, coupled with the worst breath imaginable and the occasional blood in his shit. Whisky shits were simply dreadful, but the ability to walk around and function the next day was almost pleasant. However a few bottles of red wine, cheap red wine at that, coupled with an early morning and no sleep, left Saul a wretch.

He climbed into his car and drove off to his apartment, he had enough time to go back and at least brush his teeth, maybe make some fried eggs, maybe vomit in the shower. The shower was unlikely. As he drove the short distance to his apartment he began to think about the daily time log, about the multiple required signing-ins, everything that lay ahead for him for the day. A feeling of overwhelming despair suddenly filled him. He saw in the adjacent cars clean people who probably hadn't spent the night up drinking, driving cars they took the time to vacuum and wash, wearing pressed shirts. Saul could see the whiteness of some of these guys' shirt collars through their tinted windows. Fuck me thought Saul, here he was wondering if he should tint his own windows a few shades darker.

As Saul reached his apartment he climbed the stairs. He was using the hand rail, he was actually holding on. He needed it. He was like an old man pulling himself, willing himself not to fall over and break his fucking hip. What was he going to be like when he was sixty? Again he imagined every other musician in the world who played a gig last night. Was Bono getting up at six in the morning, three hours sleep behind him to go to work in an office, holding on to a hand rail to climb a few steps? Even local musicians, they would be in bed, asleep, recovering. Not

Saul though, he was off to work, he was off to put his exhausted foot in his other world.

Saul made it to his door. He saw the woman upstairs walk down her own steps and pass him by without looking up. She was off to her work, she wore a dark blue dress suit. It was ferociously blue, it had black trimming. It made her look incredibly dumpy. She looked like a bulldog or a tank or an English pillar box, only blue, and with arms and legs and a mean face. She walked like a bulldog too, her right shoulder dipped a little and held forward. Her heels clapping off the ground as she strode on. A jet black handbag with gold trim hung over her left shoulder. Maybe holding napalm, or poison or batteries. Wherever she was going, she looked as if she was going to make someone very unhappy.

Saul closed the door behind him, threw his keys on the kitchen table. The curtains were all closed, it was dark and cool inside. Instantly his head seemed to ease a little. His guts gave an inch or two. He opened the fridge, took out two eggs. Brought the toaster up from under the cupboard, bread in but not pushed down. Saul had become a master at cooking a well-timed breakfast. He made his fried eggs a special way, a way which he was quite proud of. First he would dice an onion, brown, white or red, but preferably red, until he had about a full saucer's worth diced up nicely. He would put the onion on a small frying pan with olive oil. He would cook the onions for about a minute sometimes adding a little garlic or chopped chilli. Then he would crack an egg on top of the onions. The egg would spill in between all the tiny gaps between the diced onion and cook slowly, the onions themselves would crisp slightly and stick to the egg, these would go on the toast which was spread with avocado, some cracked salt and pepper, and Saul would go to heaven.

He watched his onions cook in the pan. He was glad he had

run into Pat, he hoped he could learn more about that smile of his. He reached for an egg, tapped it on the side of the pan. When he cracked it over his precious onions the egg spilt like mucus and spittle and ran bloody red and rotting over the pan. He felt old cheap cabernet fill his throat, he ran to the bathroom and emptied himself into the toilet. As he did he thought about the woman upstairs, he thought about the Russian sailors and their choreography, the creeping orange feeling of the warm sick crawling back up his throat, the taste of bile in his mouth and that rancid bloodied egg.

Saul stood up, flushed the toilet. He called in sick.

He awoke about five in the afternoon, the phone was ringing. It was Pat. He was doing a photo shoot later that night for a hat company but the model had pulled out. Pat asked Saul if he would fill in, he was mainly going to be in shadow so he wouldn't have to do much. Pat just needed someone with a similar build. Saul was very nervous around cameras. He had a fear of something being caught for eternity, something he could never talk his way out of or say didn't happen like that because it would be on film. They would have proof, the world would have proof of who he was, and that was something Saul believed they should never have.

Pat said they were going to pay the model $300. Saul told Pat he got very nervous around cameras, Pat said he'd be fine. Saul agreed, Pat said he'd pick him up at seven.

It was 6:30 p.m. Saul was getting nervous about the photo shoot, he wasn't sure exactly what he was going to have to do. He imagined being dressed up in ridiculous hats being asked to do stupid poses, smiling poses, smiles which suggested the hat was the very source of the happiness. What the fuck was Pat thinking asking him to do this? He had had a few beers while he was waiting. Generally if he slept all day, which was rare, he would wake with a feeling of anxiety. A wasted day. Adding the photo shoot to this was making Saul feel very uneasy indeed. The first sight he had seen when he got up was the mess he had left in the kitchen. He couldn't risk even looking at the egg again, he picked the pan off the stove and threw it in the bin. He drank a few more beers, had one shot of whisky and put two bottles of red wine in a carrier bag to take along.

Pat beeped his horn outside. Saul took another slug from the whisky bottle, took six beers in his coat pockets and another six into his wine bag. He hurried down the stairs; the booze had settled his nerves a little. The cool air of the evening laid a soothing pass over his whole body. He jumped in the passenger side. Pat gave him a little side glance. Saul drank. Pat drove.

As they drove Pat told Saul the nature of the shoot and why it was at night time. They were heading a little distance out in the hills areas. They were going to be shooting an ad for the Akubra Hat Company. Akubra was the hat of cattlemen, jackaroos and boundary riders. So they were going to go a little out bush. Pat had the costume in the back of the car, the full regalia, checked shirt, denim jeans, knee-high boots, long brown oilskin coat and of course an Akubra hat. They would be meeting up with the brother of the ad agency who owned property out in the hills and who also would be providing the long barrelled shotgun that Akubra insisted be used. The plan was to dress Saul up, load him up with the shotgun, then put him in front of a ten foot tall grass tree and then set it on fire. All Saul had to do was stand in front, put his head down a little, and the costume, fire and shotgun would take care of the rest.

The drive out to the property was about one hour and twenty minutes. Saul was getting more nervous and a little drunk. Every time he opened another beer he offered one to Pat, Pat kept saying no, and each time his answer was shorter. They eventually rolled and banged up the driveway to the property.

Pat beeped his horn again, Saul thought it a little rude, he had done it at his place as well. When the light came on closer to the house, they could see the farmer, he waved them in. Saul put the last five beers in his pockets, grabbed his wine bag and got changed.

'Okay,' said Pat, 'let's get this thing done.'

The farmer didn't say too much, he shook hands with Pat and talked a little, pointing off into the distance while Saul was getting changed. Saul appeared from behind the car in his full outfit. He looked remarkably like the farmer, except for the oilskin. The farmer gave him a broad smile, a wink and stuck out his hand.

'Now that looks the part, let's have a quick drink before we get out there, it's a short drive to the spot and she's more than likely going to drop down to freezing along the way.'

They all headed into the farmhouse. It was quite modern inside. Big open living area, a roaring pot-belly stoked with wood; the floor was half-marble half-slate. They followed the farmer into the kitchen. There was a wine bottle nearly empty sitting next to a single glass. The farmer disappeared into a small room off the side of the kitchen. Pat was unpacking his cameras and was setting up. Saul stood in the kitchen sipping away on his beer. The house was very quiet; the thick brick kept out all sounds from outside. There was no one else in the house. The farmer must live here alone.

The farmer was gone a little while. Saul opened another beer. Pat was playing with some light meters and testing his flash. Saul was feeling a little uncomfortable around Pat at the moment, he seemed to have been irritated by Saul's drinking. Fuck him thought Saul. Drag me up here to do something I'm not comfortable with and then start giving me the cold shoulder. Saul picked up the half-glass of wine from the farmer's table when Pat wasn't looking and necked it. The farmer drank good fucking wine. The farmer reappeared into the kitchen. Saul noticed his legs were slightly unsteady, he seemed to misjudge the turn from the other room. He corrected himself expertly but Saul had seen it, and it relaxed him. A warm soothing fog started to swell up inside. The farmer was holding another bottle of wine.

He grabbed three glasses from a cupboard and put them roughly down on the table, announcing he had been saving this particular bottle for a special occasion. The farmer didn't notice the empty glass Saul had finished or if he did he didn't seem to care. Saul listened as the farmer told the obligatory story about where the wine came from, where he found it and how long he had been saving it. The farmer's face looked older in the light of the kitchen. Saul could tell he was excited to have the photo shoot up on his property.

'I hope you boys both enjoy good wine.'

'He's not drinking.' Saul gestured to Pat who was now finished setting up and was approaching the table.

'I'll take a half-glass,' said Pat politely.

Mother-fucker thought Saul, here is a man opening up his prized bottle with a giving heart and this little prick asks for half a glass. Saul felt like picking up the near-empty bottle and smashing it across Pat's face.

Saul watched as the farmer took a long draught from his wine. If the farmer wasn't drunk before, he was now. Pat had not spoken to Saul since they pulled up out front. Saul listened as Pat tried to engage the farmer on a professional level.

'I'd imagine the landscape here lends itself beautifully towards photography during the daylight hours?

'Were you always from the hills or did you come out here for work?

'What sort of farming is it that you do out here exactly?'

The farmer looked disappointedly at Pat and gave him the

stock answers required of the questions. The farmer looked terribly lonely. He looked like he wanted to talk about where he found his wine, how long he had been collecting wine, which wine he first fell in love with, how did it make him feel. He looked like he wanted to share his thoughts and sorrows and dreams, if he had any left, with someone, especially these two young men who came up to see him tonight. He was trying to find some magic left in him and share it, but Pat was making it very hard.

After the farmer and Saul had finished their glasses and Pat had taken one sip out of his half, they headed outside to take the photos.

'I'll just get my gun,' the farmer said, again disappearing into another room. Saul let Pat walk out ahead, Saul stayed behind and drank the rest of Pat's glass. The farmer came back, this time with a long leather satchel slung over his shoulder. Saul smiled at him as he came out. The farmer smiled back, touched Saul on the back.

'Come on son, let's have some fun.'

Pat was waiting in his car with the engine on. Contemptuous little fucker. The farmer led Saul in the direction of his ute.

'Hop up there on the back and hang on tight to the roll bar.' He jumped in the driver's seat and wailed on his horn. 'Come on Pat,' he called. 'You're not getting far in that thing.'

Pat begrudgingly killed the engine in his car, opened the door and stepped out. He reached into the back seat and took out his bags of cameras. Saul thought it interesting the cameras were on the back seat. Maybe Pat still wanted him to sit up front or maybe that was for the farmer. Pat made his way to the passenger side of the ute and climbed in, didn't say a word to Saul as he did.

The ute sparked into life, its diesel engine growling, the farmer's radio had been left on and boomed out some bizarre strains of world music, maybe Brazilian, maybe Argentinean.

As the ute took off in the direction of the spot, Saul clung tight as he stood up tall, wind in his face. The farmer was right, the temperature had dropped fast. The music was driving through Saul's brain along with the beer, wine and whisky. The ute swung from left to right as it traversed the rocky pathways and dips of the bush track. It then levelled off and the ute built up its speed, someone turned the music up inside the cab, Saul guessed it wasn't Pat.

Saul jumped down from the ute onto the hard earth. The light of the moon was fairly bright and Saul could make out a run of grass trees standing well over twelve foot tall. They were sturdy black-barked trees that knobbled upwards and often ended in two prongs. Instead of leaves at the top of the tree were long strands of hard grass, some about two metres in length. They did for the Australian bush what cactus does for the American west.

'Now Saul, just stand in front of that one to your left,' Pat had set up a small blue lantern which gave enough light to make out the shapes on the ground.

Pat was talking to Saul again. He began to play with the settings on his cameras, looking through the lens, setting off the flash, moving about from different angles.

'Ok,' said Pat, 'I think we're ready for the tree now.'

'Hang on,' the farmer called, fishing for a lighter in his pockets and moving next to Saul under the tree. 'All right then,' he said with the lighter in hand, 'let's put on the party lights.'

With that the farmer walked behind Saul and held the lighter flame to the grass trees. The first spot caught fire, then he did the same on the other side of the tree. In seconds, the entire tree burst into a roaring sixteen foot ball of flame. The ground all around Saul and Pat and the farmer turned a brilliant orange, the heat from the blaze was tremendous. The grass tree raged on and Pat began clicking away on his camera and shouting directions at Saul.

'Put your left shoulder slightly forwards and look down towards your shoes.'

'Kneel down on the ground, move slightly in towards the tree.'

After thirty seconds the fire began to die down, the grass shoot had all been burnt and now the stumps of the prongs glowed, swelling in the dark.

'Right, now with the gun,' the farmer said, taking over the directions. 'Let's use this one next time.'

The farmer pointed to an even larger grass tree a few metres away. Saul headed over, the farmer unzipped his satchel and produced a long barrelled shotgun which stood nearly a metre and a half from end to end.

'I used all my blanks up last weekend scaring feral cats, so we're going live. This is how you do it: snap open, drop in the shells, snap closed, two clicks back, point, aim, bang.'

'Maybe we shouldn't load live rounds, guys,' Pat said, ducking his head out from over his camera. The farmer let off two quick shots into the night air. He reloaded it again repeating his instructions, sticking it in Saul's hands. SHELLS, SNAP, CLICK, POINT, AIM, BANG. The farmer took the lighter back out of his pocket, set the giant grass tree on fire and ran out of shot.

Again the fire roared into the air, the black-orange glow burst into the night sky. Shards of fire rained down over Saul as the giant grass tree crackled and scorched behind him. Saul could feel the barrel of the shotgun warming in his hands. He couldn't hear Pat as well as before. He turned towards the camera holding the barrels towards Pat. Pat seemed to shrink behind his camera and began walking backwards.

'Turn to the right Saul, turn to the right!' Pat was shouting now.

Saul turned his body to the right, swinging the long barrel across him. He raised the gun to the night sky, he could see the reflection of the blaze run down the double barrels stretching out towards the stars. Saul felt drunk with power, with wine, with life. The inferno behind him burned hard and hot, Saul could feel his back roasting under the heavy coat.

'Point aim bang!' screamed the farmer from somewhere in the darkness. 'Point aim bang!'

Saul pulled hard on the trigger. The first shot rocked him on his heels, he wobbled backwards off balance; the second blew him off his feet entirely into the base of the tree. Saul lay looking up at the blaze still burning, sprinkling flecks of fire over his body. He felt a glow in his heart, rocks under his back, and heard Pat shouting at the farmer who was laughing hysterically.

(From *My Dog Gave Me the Clap*, a novel, 2011.)

## JON DOUST

# TO THE HIGHLANDS

It was 1968. The world was falling apart. Bits of it were burning. In Europe, Britain and America students were running amok. In Perth they did what they always did: studied, got pissed, stumbled in and out of relationships, played tennis, went to the beach, fought, fucked, bragged about fucks that never existed, and drove cars into fences, trees and other cars. When I left school most of the kids in my year went on to university, as they should, because my old school, Grammar School for Boys, expected it, their parents expected it, they expected it. They were future leaders and had to be groomed to take over. My shocked parents did not cope well with my final exam results and my mother tried to rip my face off. Dad stepped in, pushed Mum out of the way, and gave me to the bank, Australia's first bank, The Colonial Bank of Australia. He grabbed me by the scruff of the neck and hauled me down to the local branch and said to the manager: Take him, or I'll kill him. Well, he didn't say that, but his look did.

I hated the bank. My career was a series of fits and starts. I was good with people, so my enquiry counter work was well reviewed. Numbers were not a strong point and so my stints as a batch clerk, agency teller relief and ledger examiner with responsibility for balancing the day's incomings and outgoings across the entire branch, were not well reported. My weeks were long, boring and highlighted by the daily early-morning erection. Once I was on the bus and it began its stop–start routine there was nothing I could do to stem the rising lizard. I enjoyed the sensation, and hated the embarrassment.

I wasn't alone; there were other bankers like me, failed sons on early-morning buses, battling bulging pants and wealthy middle-class parents who had spent thousands on exclusive, wasted educations. We were biding our time, waiting for an opportunity to crop up, dad to give us a job in the family business, grandfather to die and leave us a million, a mate to score us a job with his stockbroker father, or another one to fix us up with an easy job making big money with his dad's mining company, or marriage to that blonde chick, the one whose parents owned the supermarket chain.

Some mornings I woke, full of the heavy clouds from the night before, and sat there, on the end of the bed, wondering what sort of a life it was, the one I was living. I had a job I detested, worked with people who bored the shit out of me, like the accountant in the Gosnells branch who insisted on talking to me about farm machinery because he grew up on a farm and he once met my dad and I couldn't say anything like you're a knob, mate, and you're giving me the shits because if I did he might give me a bad report and I'd be back working the batch clerk's job which was the most boring job in the entire banking system because all you did all day was pick up forms, stamp them, sort them and hand them over to the ledger examiner who was the next most boring person in the branch and all he wanted to talk about was English soccer because that's where he was from and when he did he talked with one of those whingeing accents that turned your blood cold and your fists hot.

Dad wanted me to sit my leaving and matriculation exams again. He made me go to night-school. I hardly ever went because I knew I'd only fail again and because the two TAFE teachers looked like they belonged in a bank. Whenever I spoke to Dad or Mum on the phone, or they visited the city, all I ever got was: Why can't you be more like your brother Thomas? Or Tim Bentley, who was studying medicine, or Barbara Perkins, who was studying history? Even most of the boys in my class, the bottom class, got into university. Thomas was in university studying law. I was working in a bank. Down at the Rotary club the conversation was all about Thomas.

Someone in the back of my head kept talking to me. It might have been Jesus or the Phantom, I could never put a name to him, but he kept on at me about living a good and moral life and doing unto others as I would have done unto me and fighting injustice and defeating the communist bastards, but the voice wasn't strong enough and I found myself living the strange life of someone I didn't know, someone I had happened upon while in search of the real me.

The day I flew out to the islands, Dad had a Rotary conference to attend in Bunbury. He had to be there, not only because he was president of the Genoralup club but because he was working his way through the ranks of other club presidents and aiming to become a district governor. I drove down to see them the weekend before. As usual we sat around the kitchen table, drinking Mum's all-milk coffee brew and taking conversation leads from Dad.

I still don't think it's a good idea, said Dad. But when you come home I'd like you to give a talk at Rotary.

Sure, I said.

And remember to eat plenty of salt and take your malaria pills.

Right.

That was pretty much it. Mum cried, of course, kissed me with her lips pursed and Dad crushed my hand. Dad didn't say what he really thought and neither did I. Why would we? What good would it do? He thought I was useless and didn't believe for a minute that the bank had chosen me, that I was a chosen one, that it was grooming me for higher office. And I thought he was a prick who was determined to make sure my life was as dull and lacking in adventure as his and his Rotarian mates'. We were Grammar School boys, all of us: Dad, my older brother Thomas, and everybody who meant anything to anybody including young brother Bill who was already booked in for his high school years.

My old schoolmate, Brett Jones, picked me up and took me to Perth airport. There was a mob there to see me off. Some old school friends, a few mates from the bank, a couple of blokes from the football club and an almost, could have been, girlfriend, Megan Stirling. She was going out with a friend of mine but as soon as she saw me she would laugh. Older blokes told me that was a good sign, if a girl laughed at you, or with you, I wasn't sure which was best, or what the difference was. They said I should have a crack at her, make a move, step in, work my charm. I wasn't sure. Her boyfriend was a mate. But Megan arrived at the airport alone.

Megan had great hair. You could see she worked on her hair. She was about my height and when she walked her eyes sort of danced around and her hips kind of swayed and her legs formed calves. I loved a leg with a calf. When I was in high school I was desperately in love with the well-calved Sandra Johnston who was interschool one hundred yards champion and I wanted her calves and mine to lock and rub because I was fast too and my calves were strong and well defined but I wasn't a champion, only ever good enough for the relay team.

Megan liked me. I could tell by the way her eyes found mine and the way her mouth almost laughed as soon as I spoke her name: Megan Stirling, oh yes, stirling.

Everyone was pretty happy. The Orbit Inn at Perth airport seemed to have different rules to the rest of the city. The beers flowed over the bar and no one said: Hey you! You're underage. In West Australia the drinking age was twenty-one and I couldn't wait to get to the islands because there the drinking age was the same as in Victoria and New South Wales, eighteen. If the drinking age was eighteen, I reckoned it probably meant a lot of other things were possible too, like the things you'd heard about Sydney, Sin City, and other things, things I hadn't thought of, things I had thought of but was too shy or afraid to mention, and things that were impossible anywhere else on earth.

As all the blokes pushed me towards the departure gate, stumbling and dropping my carry-on luggage, Megan came up behind me and put her arms around me. I turned my face into her face and we kissed, full on. The blokes yelled and whistled but we kept on kissing and I could feel my pants tighten due to the lizard growing inside them. When she let my lips go she whispered in my ear: We should have done that ages ago. My face got hot and red and I pretended to stumble again and the sound of her laughter only encouraged the lizard and so I ran away to the gate that led to the plane that led to Sydney where I caught the next plane that led to the islands.

Hey, yelled a man at my door.

Jesus! You scared the shit out of me.

Yeah, he said, you me too. Gidday, I'm Ted Robinson. From Brisbane.

What are you doing here?

I live in a room down the back. You must be the new bloke from Perth.

Must be. Jack Muir.

We shook hands. Ted was one of those blokes you liked, soon

as you set eyes on him. Tall, rangy, tanned, broad-shouldered, just what you'd imagine a Queenslander would look like.

Breakfast?

Huh? Yeah. Where?

Up the new mess. Didn't anyone tell you anything? I've got a motorbike. I'll give you a lift.

You think I should put my pants on?

Ha ha. Might as well. The sheilas up there aren't worth leaving them off for.

Robinson rode a motorbike like you would imagine a Queenslander would, hell for leather, low around a bend, fast as Flint up a hill, zippy across an intersection, all the while talking his head off over his shoulder.

There's a good bunch of blokes in the bank, he yelled. Most nights we go to a bar over in the satellite town, Bulimbi. Some of the sheilas go too but they aren't much to look at. A big night is when a mob of mixed race tarts turn up. Oh, mate, they are something.

As he talked I kept my eyes on the road. It wasn't much of a road but I grew up in a house at the end of a gravel track, so anything with bitumen was okay by me. This road was sealed but it looked like great lumps of tar had been tossed off the back of a truck. Along the road natives walked, mostly men and some women with things sitting on or hanging off their heads. The vegetation looked sparse and dry, not the lush tropical growth I had expected.

Looks a bit dry, I yelled at the back of Robinson's head.

Won't be long, he yelled back. The wet season'll get underway any minute.

When Robinson turned his bike off in the new bank mess driveway, he stood beside his Honda Black Bomber and said: What do you reckon?

Nice bike, I said.

I love it and there's one more thing I gotta have before I leave this bloody place.

What's that?

A trip to the Islands of Love.

What?

You never heard of them?

Nuh.

They're on the other side of the main island. I know blokes who've been there. They reckon you just walk up to sheilas, ask for a fuck and if they like the look of you, you're in. Sex is just a game for them.

You're joking.

Nuh. You interested?

Of course I was, but I didn't say it out loud. I wanted sex, I was clear about that, but I was still a virgin, and still a bit scared of the wrath of a God who was no longer with me, or didn't exist. Then there was the wrath of a mother who believed that sex was created by the Heavenly Man so we could reproduce, and fucking for fun was a sin and deserving of retribution.

The dining room was nothing like my old boarding school dining room. It was like a large restaurant with modern chairs, tables, no prefects at their heads, all very civilised. People lined up for food served by native men through a servery. The furniture and general decor was plain and functional but the view out the large windows and across the bay was spectacular.

Come on, Jacky, let's get food, said Robinson. After breakfast I'll take you down to the bank and we'll see if we can't get the day off to ride you around town.

As people passed us they said: Gidday, Robbo. And: What are you up to, Robbo? Then: You already corrupted the new bloke, Robbo? Finally: Jesus, Robbo, haven't they sent you home yet?

Right after breakfast, we walked into the main branch of the bank. It sat on the ground floor of the two-storey building, just below the old quarters where Robbo and I lived as the only occupants.

You better come meet the branch accountant, said Robbo. He said he knows you. He's a West Aussie too.

There was no need to find his office, Richard Symons was already out of it and walking towards us. That must have been why I got the job, my big break in the banking world, because Symons had headed the two bank training schools back in Perth, the two schools where Jack Muir shone, rose above the pack. There you are, Jack, said Symons. Good to see you again. How was your flight?

Great, Mr Symons, I said. It was a long flight but I managed to stay above ground.

You still have your sense of humour, Jack. That's good, you'll need it here. And, by the way, we are not as formal in the islands, so, please, call me Richard.

Thanks, Richard, I will.

Ted here has asked that you two have the day off so he can show you around town. Are you happy with that arrangement?

Sure, I'm just not so sure about his bike riding.

No one is, said Symons. But look, let's make it half a day off, because I want you to come back here to see what we have in store for you. Given your knowledge and intelligence, we have quite a challenge for you and I believe you are up to it.

Gee, thanks, Richard. Okay.

Robbo lifted his eyebrows at me as we walked out the main entrance, past two neatly dressed white girls. I almost missed them because I was going over Symons' words.

Deep inside me there was a small part making noises, maybe wanting to believe in me and hoping to show the disbelievers back home that I had something, could do something, if I wanted to, if I felt like it. The old headmaster. Dad. Mum. My brothers. It would be a new experience, to make good; I'd have to stay focused, to concentrate, to dedicate, to strive for consistency. I felt nervous, anxious, but ready. I decided to buy some salt to keep in my room because salt would help me keep my cool. When I was a kid I was diagnosed with pinks disease, mercury poisoning, and the family doctor reckoned salt would help me stay calm. I wasn't sure, I still experienced sudden rushes of anxiety, but I loved salt and most days ate a handful of the stuff. And when drinking I couldn't keep my hands off the beer nuts and the potato chips.

I laughed out loud.

What? said Robbo.

Symons, I said. Did you hear what he said about me?

Yeah, he's got the hots for you.

Ha ha. You got any idea what he has in mind?

Nuh, but I'd keep your pants on at night and maybe rig up a piece of string and some tin cans, so if he comes into your room you'll hear him before he gets to your bed.

Shut up you filthy bastard. Get on your bike. Let's go see some naked ladies.

The capital looked like a frontier town, a town struggling to find itself in a maze of buildings randomly erected. Robbo rode around it like he owned it, yelling over his head and occasionally whistling at attractive mixed race girls. It might have been 1968 but there was no sign of it here, no hippies and no bearded students marching against colonialism, capitalism, fascism or calling for free love. Not all the white people wore white but they were all neatly dressed and behaving in an orderly manner.

Do you play footy? he yelled.

Which one?

Aerial ping-pong, you wanker. You sandgropers only know how to play one.

It's a better game than chimp footy.

What?

Chimp footy. You play an ape's game.

Robbo took both his hands off the handlebars and made like a chimp, just for a second, but long enough for my guts to hit my throat.

There were no naked ladies in town that day, but Robinson took me up a hill to see the sights from high, then down the hill and across town to the place we would visit often at night in many futile attempts to find the perfect mix of feminine beauty: Melanesian, European and Asian. When I say futile, I don't mean ladies approaching perfection did not visit, they did, but they were usually on the arm of some flash, rich, or important, prick.

My first day in teller's box number two almost convinced me I had a career in banking. I felt like the new Australian prime minister, John Gorton, who had been elected PM even though he was a senator and thus a member of the wrong house of parliament. Here I was wrongly appointed well above my capabilities, to a teller's box I didn't belong in, with a float of fifty thousand dollars, more money than I'd ever seen. I shared the box with Tom Hallett, the bloke leaving, going home after his two-year tour of duty. That's what we called it. National Service was in full force in Australia and to do your time in the islands you had to apply for a stay on your conscription papers. As soon as I headed home I'd have to let the defence department know and it would chuck my marble in the barrel and that could mean another tour of duty in another tropical climate fighting slimy Viet Cong communist bastards. Hallett was going in the barrel as soon as he got home to Melbourne. He was a tall, good-looking man and an Aussie Rules footballer. If his marble came out, he was sure to go to Vietnam.

I play for one of the local teams, he said. You interested in a game?

Yeah, maybe, I said. I wasn't too bad in school and I played a few amateur games in Perth but I'm a bit off the boil.

I'll take you down to training one night and you can see how you go.

Great.

The day was a blur. As soon as the doors opened the customer tide rushed in and didn't go out until the doors closed. All kinds trooped up to the counter: wealthy whites, drunk whites, whites in whites, whites in suits, handsome whites, very pretty whites, glorious looking blacks, blacks in whites, blacks in skirts with naked breasts, blacks with bones in their noses, blacks who stank and blacks who looked at me as though I was some kind of film star. All the while Hallett stood beside me and commented.

You see that bloke, he's worth a million. She's been around. Phil's played Rugby League down in Sydney. I saw her the other night, after the footy game, mate, she scrubs up well. Whatever you do, don't lick your fingers when counting the notes, you never know where these maries have kept their money.

What?

Yeah, that's what they call the women—maries, said Hallett. They're all called Mary and they keep their notes up their fannies.

You're bloody joking.

Nuh. You see that one down the end of the line? After you count her notes you better go and wash your hands.

I started with fifty thousand dollars, I took in over forty thousand and I handed out over twenty-five thousand and, at the end of the day, I balanced. I couldn't believe it. The old man couldn't believe it. Okay, he wasn't there, but I felt him breathing down the back of my neck, waiting for me to fuck up, to lose count, to mess the numbers up, but I didn't and inside I said a quick, silent, fuck you, you prick.

My little teller door opened. I turned and saw Symons. His hand was out, looking for mine.

There you go, he said. I had plenty of confidence in your ability to master this position. I knew you'd handle it. Knew you wouldn't let us down.

Phew, I said. Good to know I'm no John McEwen.

Symons looked at me.

You know, forced to take charge because someone died, but the wrong man for the job.

Would have been better to shove in Billy Big Ears McMahon, said Hallett. Billy might not be up for the top job either, but looking at his wife would make up for it.

McMahon had not long married a delicious woman twenty-five years younger than him and the best looking politician's wife ever. No one could explain how such a big-eared dill got to marry such a beauty, especially after so many thought he was a poofter. And no one could explain why I was still a virgin in a world gone mad with promiscuity. Not that anyone knew. It was my pathetic little secret. Along with all the others, like the lingering, occasional conversation I had with Jesus and the reason I ate so much salt.

What a day, that first one in the second teller's box. I was pumped. I needed a drink. That's the way to make euphoria last: you win a game, you get engaged, you win money, you get a pay rise—you go out and get pissed. Sober, euphoria only lasts a couple of minutes; pissed, it lasts for hours. That's what it was to be Australian. I had begun to think of myself as Australian, as belonging to a nation of people. I wondered if it had happened to the other expats, if before they had arrived they had considered themselves Queenslanders, or Victorians, but once away from our island continent, they began to think of themselves as Australians.

That whole first week in the teller's box was sweet and amazing. One night I also had another one of my flying dreams. A good one. They aren't always pleasant and sometimes I can't seem to get off the ground, no matter how hard I frog-kick or stroke with my arms. That's how I move through the air, with the breaststroke kick and stroke. It never ceases to amaze me how I do it. I never see anyone else up there with me. People look up and wave or try to get at me but they never get off the ground. In this dream I was shooting through the air, just flying, feeling the air, doing a few rolls, having fun. And when I came down Mum was waiting for me with the evening meal. She watched me land but she didn't look surprised and didn't say anything other than: Dinner's ready. I looked around for Dad but he wasn't there.

I couldn't believe how well everything was going. Everywhere. In Perth, the greatest Aussie Rules footballer ever, Polly Farmer, was back home and appointed captain-coach of West Perth; my brother Thomas was working in Perth as a lawyer; brother Bill was winning races and looking to be a future athletics champion; Dad had opened a new business in the town next door; and here I was straining at the bit, biting at the rope, wondering what to do now I had conquered the second teller's box. This was turning out to be my best year ever. There had to be more and bigger, brighter, better things out there for me to take on, here in the islands, at home, Europe, America, England. The world was my oyster. Maybe this was where it all started and then I'd move on to even greater success, eventually returning home triumphant: the prodigal son knocks on the door at the end of the gravel driveway, but not alone, he comes with fame, fortune and prestige, a wife, a great bundle of things they never imagined. Mum will cry, of course. Dad will look at me, in disbelief, amazement, stand back, take another look, have a think about it, check out my wife, be very impressed, then he will walk up to me, perhaps give me a traditional Italian greeting, a big man-hug with hands slapping my back. Even Jesus will weep then. What? What's he got to do with it? Shut the fuck up about Jesus. He doesn't exist, or maybe he does but not as the son of God, more likely a bloke like Gandhi, the Dalai Lama, or Herb Elliott. The longer I lived the more it looked like there was no God, but in a little piece of my brain, somewhere up the back, every so often, a conversation took place and I kept thinking it might be Jesus. Maybe I just needed someone to talk to and he was the only bloke available, even though he wasn't.

Surely Dad wouldn't be surprised by my current burst of success; after all he sent me to Grammar School. Grammar boys were destined for greatness, leadership, wealth, that was their birthright, their destiny. And look at me now, surging ahead, things appearing at my feet with very little effort. Even a mixed race girl of astonishing beauty was coming into the bank, eyeing me off, laughing at my little jokes. Maybe it was time to find out her name.

That first week in the second teller's box was a revelation. I had no idea I could handle so much money, or even that I could handle money. When I wrote home I made no mention of my success. On the Friday night we all went over to the Pacific Hotel and drank like dogs in a spring after a run in a desert, and then I walked back to my little cockroach-infested room drunk, so drunk I slept the entire night in my designated room, the room without the massive ceiling fan and the stored documents. When I woke up at three a.m. to piss, I got a shock, I thought I was back home, in Genoralup, and I wondered why the room was facing the wrong way, why it was hot, so muggy, and my arm was a mass of bulging mosquitoes on heat and what were those soft noises like tiny things scratching? By the time I got to the toilet, I remembered. And when I got back to the room I decided to leave the cockroaches to my underpants, the mosquitoes to Robbo down the hall, and shift back to the paperwork and the fan.

The sad thing about getting pissed on a Friday night was that you had to get up again on Saturday morning and work until midday. Then, of course, unless you played sport, you could go off and get pissed again. My Saturday in the teller's box was marred by a small error. I finished the day fifty dollars over, but I was forgiven quickly, because I was over and not under and because fifty dollars in a float of fifty thousand was not deemed a disaster.

The next week was another major success, except I was getting a little bored. Life seemed to be all about work. You got up, you went to breakfast, you went to work, you bought lunch, you worked, you closed the doors, you went to your room, you went to dinner, you went out and got a little pissed, you went to bed. If you got a little too pissed you might have to get up and chuck your guts, you got up, chucked them, and on and on it went until you died and the mosquitoes sucked the last of your blood and the cockroaches consumed what was left and thirty-five years later someone noticed you were missing, went upstairs to the old document storage room and found your clothes and a letter from your mother reminding you to eat plenty of salt because you were once diagnosed with mercury poisoning.

By the third week the boredom was getting to me. The mixed race girl at Friday night rugby was still only smiling at me, laughing at an occasional comment, but not inviting me to share her secrets, her bed or her vagina, and my old school chum Bainbridge was about to leave town and go south.

There was a football match each week, the Aussie Rules game on Sunday. I went down to one training session for a look at a practice match but the sight of one local, built like a brick outhouse, roaring into one of the pasty white blokes was enough to make me flinch twice, then think. The game seemed to be a mix of rugby and Aussie Rules, some finesse, an occasional high mark, but a lot of punching, kicking, shoving in scrums and bashing, smashing, running as though their lives depended on the ball under their arms. I enjoyed it, but it wasn't like the game I knew and of the codes on offer I preferred the raw and brutal honesty of Rugby League. But when you're away from home you get all the entertainment you can and so I went to all games.

One Sunday, right after the booze-up in the clubrooms, six of us squeezed ourselves into the Volkswagen of the Bulimbi branch accountant. Jim Jackson was an older man, an alcoholic and, naturally enough, more often than not, pissed. He drove like he was pissed. What did we care? We were members of an expatriate community and expats driving pissed was normal. For most of us there was no other way to drive.

You right there? called a South Australian from the back.

The croweater, Roger, sat in the middle of the back seat. I sat on the outside, the left side, the side facing the bay, and Robbo sat on the right side, looking up the cliff face. In the front were two Victorians and Jackson at the wheel. It was a narrow road around the bay linking Bulimbi with the centre of the capital.

Too bloody right, said Jackson.

The road was wet and the rain hadn't stopped for two hours. Jackson was taking us back to the old bank quarters. Robbo and I were going out later that night to the Bulimbi Bar. My old school mate Bainers was playing his last gig and he had a hot, new, mixed race drummer in the line-up. This was a good thing and the night might well attract the drummer's sisters, their friends and their friends.

Jim was driving like a sober man. We were all laughing. All was well with the world.

You all right up front? yelled Robbo.

Too bloody right, yelled Jackson.

Jackson turned his head to show us the laughter on his face, but he turned too far, lost concentration, took a bend a little too tight, tried to correct, overcorrected, just missed an oncoming Volkswagen, overcorrected again and headed for the edge. We might have been pissed but we all knew the edge was not a good place to be. We yelled at Jackson, not so much because of the edge itself, more because after the edge there was nothing for a good twenty feet and at the bottom of the fall, on the bay floor, there was nothing but rock and an incoming tide.

Jim, yelled Robbo, we're on the fucking edge.

We hung there. No one really thought that we would go over and it looked like we wouldn't, then it did, then it didn't and then Jackson made a strange noise from his throat and his hands seemed to leave the wheel, then they took it again but moved in the wrong direction. The car shook. There was uncertainty about how much of us was on the edge, or over it. One wheel? Or two? I was sure the wheel under me was over, had been for a second or two. We seemed to hang for a long time, then a small shift, then, ever so slowly, we fell. The fall was nice. I enjoyed the fall. It was almost like flying. Someone screamed, a woman, and it was then I realised that one of the Victorians in the front was a woman. Lucky for her she was in the middle, over the handbrake. The other Victorian, Nigel, was in front of me and as the car fell I thought, shit, I better put my elbow on the roof or a rock will come in through the window and smash my arm to smithereens, and in just the amount of time it took to think that and do it, a rock appeared at my armpit. Nigel and the Victorian woman next to him screamed, Robbo yelled, the croweater between us screamed and Jackson was silent.

On the bottom of the bay, moving quickly was important because the tide was coming in fast as it always did and lying there in a smashed Volkswagen was not a good idea. Robbo yelled at Jackson to open his door. Jackson sat slumped, gurgling.

Jackson, I yelled. For fuck's sake move.

Robbo reached over him, opened his door, pushed his seat forward then climbed out over him. Roger the croweater followed. From inside the car I helped them lift, pull and push Jackson out. He was sobbing and blubbering, apologising to everyone and offering to buy us all a drink when we got out and even take us all out for a meal. The Victorians in the front were next out and in no mood for either drink or food. The woman was helping Nigel, who was no longer screaming but moaning.

It's all right, Jim, said Robbo. Come on, we gotta get out of here because the tide's coming in and we have to get Nigel to hospital. His arm is cut up pretty bad.

Nigel's arm was in threads and blood was leaving his body in gallons whichever way he turned. The front passenger door looked like it had aimed itself for the biggest rock and most of his arm must have been on it because there wasn't much left of it where it used to be.

Here, I said, take my shirt.

The woman took my shirt and I helped her tear off a strip.

Thank you, she said. I'm June, by the way.

Great place to meet people, I thought, climbing out of a drunk Volkswagen crashed on an ocean bed with a tide racing in. I looked at her then and she wasn't too bad at all.

I'm Jack, I said, from WA.

I know. Here, help me wrap Nigel.

We wrapped the still-moaning Nigel and helped him walk across the rocks towards a place where the road and the bay bed were much closer together and where people had found a way down and were walking towards us. By now vehicles had stopped above us and some were calling out.

My wife has gone to get an ambulance, yelled a man.

Three men who had climbed down into the bay were almost

with us. When they reached June and Nigel they took him back the way they had come. June turned back and grabbed at my arm.

You're hurt, she said.

No, not me.

But look.

I looked down at my arm and saw the blood and the deep cut.

Arrr, it's nothing.

What, so you West Aussies are tough, are you? Can't feel a thing, huh?

She poked her finger at the blood and I yelped.

So, you wanna go for a drink later then?

Crikey, she said. What a time to ask a girl out.

When she smiled her entire face moved, her eyebrows lifted almost to her hairline and her upper body rocked. I thought: Maybe. But it never happened. What did happen, of course, was we all went to hospital, got stitched, bandaged, released, all except Nigel, were interviewed by the police, caught a taxi to the Pacific Hotel and got so pissed we had to catch another taxi home, even though we only lived across the road. I didn't sleep that night, because not long after I went to bed I had to get up and throw everything I had eaten or drunk over the past week into the shower recess. It stank. I stank. When I arrived at work the next morning, I stank still.

(From *To the Highlands*, a novel, 2012.)

# MARTIN CHAMBERS

# THE PIT

Spanner, Cookie and I had been on Palmenter Station the longest. We were the old hands and knew a few things we preferred not to but it was Cookie who seemed best able to ignore it all.

It was morning, just after breakfast. A muster and import had finished a few days ago and we were all relaxing. Arif and I were in the canteen, him talking at me, and me pretending to listen. Charles and Simms were there too. Spanner was down in his shed and Palmenter was in the office. We heard the rumble of a car approaching on the gravel. That in itself was unusual and I stood to look out the window.

A police car drove up to the canteen building and stopped. No one got out and in each of the buildings curious eyes must have been watching for what would happen next. The police never came out here. For them to do so now, something must be serious.

'Better hide the harvest,' called Arif to Cookie who was chopping leaf in the kitchen. Arif was serious, but the joke was that an entire plantation thrived immediately out the back door.

'Someone must have been caught,' Cookie said as he came from the kitchen casually wiping his hands on his apron. He peered out the window.

Perhaps he was right: one of the previous imports had been

picked up and then said something, given up the station and Palmenter and all of us. Unlikely, but I was wondering what this would mean for me, if I'd be charged, if we'd all be charged, with people smuggling.

Palmenter admitting anything? Ha! We'd all be for it. He'd find some way of pinning it on us and getting off scot-free. I wondered what the penalty for people smuggling was. A few years jail? And here was Cookie calmly packaging up serious quantities of dope, a crime I suspected carried a far more severe penalty, again, a crime for which Palmenter would deny all knowledge and for which I could not claim innocence.

Hopefully the police had come about something else entirely but I realised suddenly how things were. The truth was I was working on a station that routinely broke the law and each day, by my silence or inaction, I became more complicit. And there was no way out, I was trapped. I should go and get in the police car, lock myself in it and tell them to take me away.

But life is not that simple. Palmenter was a bully, an arrogant bastard, he was a ruthless money-hungry opportunist preying on the weak and dispossessed. Yet the people we were helping had no choice and at least they now had a chance at a new life, a better life, and I wasn't going to be the one to end that hope. I wanted to get away from the station, but I had to do it on my own terms.

Palmenter strolled over to the car and two policemen got out and I could hear friendly deep voices, laughter, howdyados, as Palmenter led them towards us. We drifted like ghosts back into the kitchen as they came in the canteen door. Palmenter opened beers for them at the bar while we listened from behind the swing doors.

'We hardly ever see you out this way. Don't be strangers, always a meal or a beer here for you. Anytime.'

I couldn't make out the reply because just then the freezer

motor started up. Cookie scurried out to turn it off. Last thing Palmenter wanted was cops dropping by unannounced, so him telling them not to be strangers, to drop by for a feed and a drink anytime, that was plain bullshit. I wondered if there was more going on here. It was a bit much to believe that boats could land and helicopters fly between the coast and here and not be seen. At some time someone must have reported something and Palmenter was most likely paying off the cops to keep them quiet. Probably only as a precaution. It wouldn't be too hard to turn a blind eye when your patch is one hundred thousand square kilometres.

We had crowded closer to hear better when Cookie came in from killing the freezer motor, slamming the door. We all jumped and he laughed and instead of joining us he continued to chop and wrap the crop. He neatened it into piles that he wrapped in alfoil the size of a half brick and then put all but two of them into the freezer.

'Youse lot, garn, get outta here. See my illegal activity.' But he didn't mean it. He laughed then stood at the swing doors with the rest of us, weighing the packets in his hands in a way that made it obvious that this was for the coppers.

'I'll sort it, Trent. Be gone by morning. It's all over, no problems.' Palmenter stood, dragging his chair noisily. 'You want some steaks. We just finished the muster, killed a couple.' I didn't hear an answer. 'Plenty there, I'll get you both a package,' and before any of us could move he was in the kitchen, glaring at us.

'Get some fucking steaks for these boys. Where's Spanner. Shit, he's going to pay for this. This will cost us, boys.' No one had moved. 'Fucking steaks, NOW.' Not loud. Meaningful. Cookie handed him the package and sprinted into the freezer. Palmenter pointed to me and Simms.

'You two, soon as they've gone, at the machine shed. And get fucking Spanner. Sober. The rest of you, get outta here. Go find something useful to do.'

I found Spanner in the generator shed where he was changing the oil in the second generator. He had earmuffs on and so I signalled him to come outside. He shook his head and pointed at the machine, but I insisted. He followed me out.

'What?'

I told him about the police car and what we had seen, and that Palmenter wanted us all right away. We walked around to the shed where Palmenter was already waiting with Simms. Spanner was muttering under his breath, 'This is not gunna be good.'

The van was lying on its side by the edge of the track. It was one of the seven-seaters. They are more difficult to control on the softer tracks, but what had caused them to leave the highway and venture out here we would never know. What made them crash? Could have been a roo, suddenly jumping out. They had no experience of Australian wildlife. It wasn't a blowout.

Spanner swore nothing was wrong with the van. Steering, brakes were perfect. He serviced each of the vans thoroughly before they left the station. He might not have been one hundred per cent behind the operation but he knew as well as all of us that if the van broke down on its way to the city, if the people got into trouble, most likely someone would start asking questions. Spanner had built a nice little retreat for himself here at the station. He seemed happy enough to spend his days alone in the shed and drinking a steady supply of free beer, sleeping it off from early evening and then doing it all again the next day.

They must have survived for some time. They had propped the rear door open and set up the mattresses inside. One body lay in there, shiny plastic-looking and bloated. A tarpaulin was tied between the wheels and angled with string to some shrubs.

The cooker, boxes and suitcases were arranged in the lean-to and two people were leaning against the van, looking as if they were resting, except for the flies around their faces. Empty water containers were scattered around and we could imagine the slow-rising dread and the increasing thirst. The desert heat. Flies buzzed around the bodies and the open tins of food. We followed a network of footprints to another body that lay under a shrub a short distance away. Maggots crawled in open wounds. A few metres further a shallow grave had been dug up by dingoes. Half-eaten bits of body and clothing protruded. Must have been the first to die. A frypan and a pot lay nearby and I could see them weakly trying to dig a hole with the utensils, to bury their friend with the dignity he deserved. The first one to succumb to the heat and thirst. Was he their friend? I knew that many of them ended up travelling together with nothing in common but the desire to move to a new country. Thrown together by circumstance, by a small boat and even smaller van, now burying someone they might not even know the name of, but knowing that all too soon it might be them.

'How many in this van?' asked Palmenter.

'Dunno,' said Simms.

Palmenter hit him. He swung his arm full-length and caught Simms on the jaw. Not hard, but deliberate.

'What the fuck, don't know,' he yelled. 'It's your job to know.'

'You said not to write anything down.'

Palmenter hit him again, this time hard enough to knock Simms to the ground. 'You remember. Don't write it down. How hard is it to remember?' He looked around at the scrub. 'We got to know if this is all of them.'

'Five, boss,' I said. I had no idea, but then neither did he. He looked at me. Spanner had moved away when Palmenter hit Simms but I stood my ground. 'Five. This was the last van to leave, I remember it had five.'

No such thing, I made it up but it must have sounded believable. I had counted five bodies and I did not want to spend any longer here scouting around for more. Palmenter grunted.

'Well done, at least someone's got a brain. All right then. Spanner, get a rope on it to pull it back up. You two,' Simms and me, 'put the bodies in the back. Quick smart. Lucky for us no one is ever going to miss these blokes.'

We dragged the bodies into the van. We had to climb inside, then back over them to get out, but it would have seemed disrespectful to just shove them in. We wanted to lay them out carefully but it was difficult as the bodies were putrid and flyblown. Simms began retching when we dragged the maggoty body from under the shrub. It had been eaten, an arm came off and although I tried to avoid looking it was impossible not to look at the face that was half-chewed and crawling. Simms was vomiting but something in me allowed me to hold my breath and keep going. I was thinking how unpredictable Palmenter might be, what he might do if we both stopped working and knelt in the sand with spit dribble, dry-retching. Spanner rigged the 4WD and pulled the van upright, then hitched up a towline.

Simms was quick to volunteer when we needed someone in the van to steer it. It might have been an attempt to redeem himself or perhaps it was to avoid being in the car with Palmenter. I couldn't tell. He kept touching his jaw and it looked more like the pathetic subservient gesture of a minion than for the soreness he might have felt. Anyway, I breathed a sigh of relief. I didn't want to be in with those five stinking bodies that, despite our reverently laying them out, had all tumbled to a mess on the floor as we righted the van.

At the pit Palmenter instructed us to unhitch the van and push it over the edge and torch it. It rolled to the bottom and parked itself remarkably, as if someone had driven it there. Palmenter stood at the top of the pit watching while we gathered a few clumps of dried spinifex and climbed down to stick them under the wheels. Spanner took off the fuel cap and drained some fuel into a tin. He splashed this around inside the van and onto the bodies, then he flipped the seat and pulled the fuel line from the motor and let it fall to the ground. Petrol began to leak out and soak into the ground.

'Stand back!' he called.

He dribbled a line of fuel and lit it. The flame marched slowly across the sand towards the van and almost went out. Simms was halfway up the slope but Spanner and I stood together watching, only metres from the flame that seemed in no hurry to arrive. I thought Spanner was going to say something about the bomb about to go off but he didn't.

'Farewell, you unlucky buggers,' he said.

By the time we got to the top of the pit we could feel the intense heat on our backs and smell blistering paint. Neither of us looked back.

On the drive back to the station Palmenter regained control.

'Good job, boys. Could have been a monumental fuck-up.'

The tension in the car was thick. Spanner was fuming because Palmenter had accused him of not fixing the van properly. I was worried what would happen if he spoke up.

'What were they doing on that road anyway?' I asked nobody. 'You need experience to drive on these sand tracks. In future we need to make sure they only go on the highway, give them a good map, maybe escort them to the turn-off.'

I often came up with useful ways to improve how we did things. Later, when Palmenter and his mates changed how we ran the operation by collecting the vans themselves and driving off-site to meet the imports, I thought it was because I had suggested it.

'You're a smart boy, Son,' said Palmenter. 'Always thinking

ahead. That's the way to do business, think ahead, plan for things.' He looked at me, then to Spanner and Simms. 'Sorry I lost it back there, boys.'

Fuckin' arsehole, I thought. Me and him. Arseholes both.

(From *How I Became the Mr Big of People Smuggling*, a novel, 2014.)

## AMANDA CURTIN

# THE SOUND OF A ROOM

The house is on death row. Two more days, according to the *Condemned* sign nailed to the lurching picket fence. Two days before estate agents bring in a team to dismantle and carry away what's salvageable—there won't be much—of the jarrah floorboards and plaster cornices, the Metters stove, the granite laundry trough, the rusted cast-iron bath. The rest will be reduced to rubble.

He'd approached the agents after hearing the news of poor Hughie's death, and they'd passed on his request to the solicitors, but no one had been able to grasp just what it was he was asking for. It was clear they thought him a time-waster, possibly unbalanced.

If he could have managed a third mortgage, he would have made an offer. But even his accountant had looked flinty at the notion of his buying a structurally unsound house with no intention of demolishing it—or altering it in any way. *What kind of fool investment is that?*

So it has come to this. To secure what he wants, he will have to steal it.

In the late hours, he takes up watch opposite the house, concealed behind a wild privet hedge that backs onto a stormwater drain. He has dressed the part. Black cargo pants. Black jacket. Black beanie on his head, pulled down low over knotted hair the colour of toast. Thin black gloves, black socks and runners. Of course, the smears of soot from the barbecue are pure melodrama. But the fact is: he does have an exceedingly white face, the result of working eighteen hours a day in sunless isolation. He'd had to do *something* about the contrast between skin and so much matt black. Providing he keeps his mouth closed, he can bleed into the night, just like a real cat burglar.

Footsteps approach. Good leather soles striking concrete, clean and sharp. His head tilts to catch the rhythm. A trifle uneven? Yes. The woman passing by favours her left, her gait pulled off centre by the heft of a briefcase. A briefcase, can you believe it, at this hour!

Ten minutes go by. Fifteen. A cat-shaped phantom ripples over a wall, a plastic bag cartwheels along the gutter with a rustling ssshhh, but it's beginning to look a safe bet that no one will see him slip across the road and round to the back verandah of the condemned house.

He listens, to make sure.

What he hears, others would call silence. The absence of definable noise. But there is no such thing as silence.

Water trickles along the open drain, altering in pitch as it gurgles around the leaves of fallen branches. Ten blocks to the west vehicles drone on the freeway, each engine contributing a cadence of its own to the muted hum. White ants move unseen within powdering pickets. A snail silvering the footpath displaces granules of dirt, making infinitesimal scuffs on the soundscape of night.

It is benign, its register reassuringly free of human notes. A perfect night for thieves, for stealing the sound of a room.

What does a room sound like? Students often ask him that. The question shows how much they have to learn, these young apprentices, about acoustics, about the nature of ambient noise. No two rooms have the same acoustic profile, he tells them, even if they are built from the same plan. What a room sounds like depends on its size and shape—the volume and configuration of air—but also on what is in it. Hard surfaces like glass and wood will bounce sound waves back and forward, prolonging reverberation. (Here he demonstrates, positioning sheets of glass and ply and masonite. He claps his hands, strikes a gong with a rubber mallet. There are always one or two students who volunteer to join in, making strangulated cries and listening in awe to the echo of their own voices.) Cloth and carpet will soak up the waves—the degree of absorption varying with the thickness and density of the materials and their placement in the room. (He makes his point using insulated panels, and heads nod appreciatively. Students enjoy a good comparison.) Minuscule gaps above lintels and around the frames of windows, cracks in walls, apertures created by fretted seals—these all allow an exchange of air between one room and another, or between a room and the world at large, a barely perceptible leakage of fugitive life: air conditioners, the scraping of hair through a comb, the singing of electricity on overhead wires. It is subtle, like breathing, but not soundless. (Some students look at him doubtfully. It doesn't sound very scientific.)

The most popular demonstration is when he selects a scene in a film and plays it for them with the soundtrack turned off. Oh yes, they all nod their heads at that one. What is a film without its dialogue? Its musical score? *And?* he prompts. The more alert suggest obvious sound effects—claps of thunder, car horns, slamming doors. But most forget what he has just been teaching them: the sounds of rooms, of spaces. Known as *atmos*, these are just as important to the film's soundtrack but are detectable only when they are absent or when they are wrong.

Atmos 14 is part of his stock in trade. He has been using it for years.

He remembers the precise moment when he walked into the living room of his ex-wife's Aunt Shelley's house. The party—a Christmas affair, sherry and rumballs and relatives on their best behaviour—was happening in the front room of the house, with its plump armchairs and antimacassars and doily-draped rosewood. He'd found the living room by mistake, opening the wrong door while looking for the bathroom. 'Tie a Yellow Ribbon Round the Old Oak Tree' was playing on the stereo two rooms away. He could hear subdued conversation and the clinking of glasses. But all of that he tuned out, arrested by the sound of the room. He gazed up, around, taking in the dimensions, and put his ear to the plasterboard wall. He walked the room's perimeter, judging ratios, gauging the shifts in ambience from door to wall, from corner to corner. He stood on a reclining chair beneath moulded cornices, hearing the air curve. Listening intently, trying to isolate each aural particularity, he bemoaned the fact that his spectrum analyser was not, for once, in the boot of the car. This space—it was a gem. With its waxed floorboards and panelled wainscot, the shabby velveteen drapes and brittle ceilings, the room had a pleasing balance, singular in its rendering, between dead and alive, dull and bright, an assemblage of aural reflections and refractions that was so, so—right.

He was seduced by the sound of the room, coveted what he heard.

His ex-wife, taut-faced, had to lead him away by the elbow half an hour later when his absence from the pleasantries in the front room had been remarked upon.

He returned next day with his gun mike and recorder to woo the steely-eyed Aunt Shelley. Feigning an air of bonhomie and charm, he explained his mission (for mission it was). Her purple glasses slipped down her nose sceptically, but he eventually managed to persuade her that recording the sound of an empty room was a perfectly everyday madness in his line of work.

The hairs on his arms quivered as he aimed the gun mike in different directions, at different elevations, hoping to capture an atmos suite whose subtle variations were as true on tape as they were in the room. What *was* it about this room? What word would describe the nebulous qualities of its appeal?

It was not until he played back the recording in the acoustic purity of the studio that he found the answer. Listening in wonder as the shiny ribbon of tape slid over the heads of the machine, he understood the value of what he had curated. If he closed his eyes, he was no longer in the cramped little booth with its overhead light bulb, its crudely lined walls of spongy tiles; he was transported to a room that could, with just the right tweaking, be every room, any room. It was a base from which to simulate a convincing soundscape of real life.

He had succeeded in capturing the sound of the ordinary.

The Atmos 14 family realised its potential almost immediately when he used it in the sound design for a ninety-minute telemovie set mostly in a suburban house. *The Prodigal Daughter* had earned him a reputation for verisimilitude and technical style. Since then he has adapted it for *A Boy Named Sam*, *The Sheridans*, *Here and There* and *The Family Way*—just a few in a catalogue of successful dramas. Since the advent of reality TV, it has proved its worth all over again. Many times over the years he had returned to re-sample the room: surprisingly, Aunt Shelley had warmed to the idea of her living room being famous (although it was a concept of fame difficult to explain to the neighbours), and even after his divorce from her niece she had been amenable to new recordings. He had relished the opportunity to expand the family of Atmos 14 variants in nuanced ways. Room with Door Open. Room with Door Closed. Room with Six Boring People Sipping Red Wine and Not Speaking (Shelley's neighbours). Room with Dog Hair on Carpet. Room with Copper Tureen of Minestrone. Room with Drooping Lilies. Room the Night Before a Wake.

After Shelley's death, and her bachelor brother Hughie's inheritance, he had continued his aural mapping with much trepidation, Hughie having waved his uninterested consent from the kitchen, a meat pie in his hand. But, incredibly, in spite of the gradual deterioration of the dwelling generally, thanks to lack of maintenance and Hughie's slovenly ways, the room remained almost true to its pre-Hughie state. This was, in no small part, because Hughie was lazy and not one for individual touches. Aunt Shelley's original furniture and furnishings had remained exactly as she left them, and the layers of dust they accumulated over time appeared to adulterate only fractionally the signal-to-noise ratios of the space. Room with Residue of Hughie.

There is something uncanny about that room, too. Last time he was there, white ants had begun to gain supremacy over the decaying abode, sweeping through front and back verandahs, buckling the uprights and sucking cellulose fibre from the floorboards. But, miraculously, they had stopped short of the living room, even though the stumps holding up the kitchen only feet away had crumbled to oblivion, causing the Metters first to list and then to sink through the subfloor. A room that stands unscathed while all else teeters around it is surely blessed, he thinks. And as though to prove the truth of its holiness, the foetid house seems to glow from within, right before his eyes.

He struggles to his feet, knees stiff from crouching, and shoulders his rucksack. The metal sockets of microphones and leads clink softly as he scurries across the road.

Sanctuary, for the girl, in this unlikely place, at least for two more days. The power has been disconnected; the water from the kitchen tap is a funny colour. There is a yellow smell that the toilet won't flush away. Fine runnels of something gritty, like sand, escape from sagging ceilings in the kitchen and bathroom. But it's a decent place to squat. No one knows she is here.

It's all hers. Even those boys on skateboards who'd circled the back verandah a few times had abandoned any ideas they might have had. One of them had approached the door and she'd held her breath on the other side. She thinks he might have broken a bone when his runners plunged through the brittle boards of the verandah. An outpouring of *fuck* and *Christ* and howling pain. It had taken two others to heft him out, help him hobble away. That was the last she'd seen of them and their paint-spattered hoodies. She has felt safe. Until now.

There is someone out there. She knows it.

From the time she was a small girl, she has been able to sense when someone is watching her. The man who waited in the kitchen for her mother to return with cigarettes; she ignored him, watched *The Road Runner*, but felt his eyes flicking at her bare feet, skinny limbs in pink pyjamas. Her uncle's slack-lidded appraisal from behind his poker hand. Teachers who suspected her of cheating, her marks unexpected from girls who looked like she did, who came from homes like hers. And Kyle's incessant surveillance. They had been friends since school, more since she moved in with him, so it hurt her, still, to think of what he'd done, what he was capable yet of doing. The betrayal cut her deepest. He knew about her life, and what he hadn't known she'd told him, trusting, but he'd used it as ammunition to break her down, keep her down. Everywhere she went, Kyle's eyes were on her. He could see through walls. For a while, she'd told herself it was paranoia to think he was following her to IGA. But then Cathy had seen him in the carpark, a flash of binoculars behind the steering wheel, aimed at her checkout. A small death when she found the hole drilled in the bathroom wall, hard to spot because of the bubbling of paint, the water-stained plaster dark with mould.

How could he have found her?

She moves through the house, hand cupped around a lighted candle, picking her way to where she has made a small nest for herself out of cushions from an old recliner, the jumper she'd brought with her in a green shopping bag, a blanket of velveteen torn from the house's curtains. It wasn't vandalism: the house was going to be pulled down; no one would care.

Weeks ago, she'd seen the house from the bus window, a man in a yellow hardhat and matching fluoro tunic picking his way carefully over the front verandah with a clipboard, a torch. Then the sign had gone up and boards across a broken window. The next day she'd got off at the closest bus stop and circled back towards the house, keeping some distance, glancing from behind sunglasses. Four times she'd walked past, noticing. There was a collapsing fence but no gate to prevent access. No close neighbours. A laneway at the rear. A quiet neighbourhood. She'd listened to the silence. Perfect.

Has he found her?

It's the only room in the house that isn't beginning to collapse in on itself, that's free of that peculiar, suffocating dust of disintegration. She wedges the candle in the hole of a broken brick and hunkers down in her nest, her back to the dark window, shaking before fear that has the contours of a man, lean and sinewy, with ropy arms and curled fists that can split skin.

Minutes pass. Nothing.

She is imagining it. Almost laughable, really, her puny self no match for the enormity of that fear. It is pathetic, what she has become.

A noise at the back door.

She moves swiftly to pinch the candle between her fingers. He has found her. Her sanctuary is being breached. The flame disappears, but a flare of anger illuminates the room.

This is *her* house.

On the back verandah he struggles with a rusty latch, a warped door. Unlocked—he'd not expected that, had come prepared with a jeweller's screwdriver, slim and pointed, and some flat paint-scraping tool he'd bought from Bunnings, imagining it might be thin enough to slip between the door frame and the plate of the lock. But here it is, the door unlocked, a gift. Beginner's luck.

As he enters the house, his hands are trembling, so intense is the anticipation of acquisition, tempered by imminent loss. For this will be the last time. He knows that what he has come to steal is the room's dying moments, the laboured breathing that precedes no breath at all. It is the final scene in the story of Atmos 14, the last nuance to be wrung from the ordinary.

He wedges open the door to the living room, puts down the torch and rucksack. Listens.

It perplexes him, the denseness, its particulate quality. The literalness of the room's breathing. As though it is unwilling to be used again, resisting in death the pliable ordinariness that has been its perfection.

*Fanciful.* Now analyse. Head to one side, he tries to identify what is different, what is wrong.

Too swift for conscious recognition, but his ears know what they are hearing: Broken Brick Cleaving Air. The sound of the room dissolving ...

(From *The Kid on the Karaoke Stage*, short fiction, 2011.)

# RON ELLIOTT

# DOUBLE OR NOTHING

*So far, hopeless gambler Dave has burnt a lot of bridges, which include in ascending order his ex-wife, his boss, the local police, his favourite Cash Converter franchisee and his bookie. When he stumbles across a case of uncut diamonds at the scene of a jeep crash in the Kimberley on the body of a man of some resemblance to his own handsome self, he decides to give the wheel of fortune a hefty spin. What could go wrong?*

Dave stood near the check-in of the Perth International Airport counting the money in the envelope for the third time. One thousand English pounds.

Dave had shown Ken's driver's licence at a pick-up counter in the airport, deciding the photo on that looked a little more like him than the one in Ken's passport. They gave him a manila envelope. Inside was an airline ticket to Amsterdam and an address. A typed note said *Go by the name of Angus MacFergus, rest of payment COD.* There was a smaller envelope containing the money.

Dave bought a carry-on bag for nineteen dollars and ninety-five cents and used his ticket and Ken's passport to get a boarding pass. As he was walking towards the security person who checked boarding passes and passports he recalled his few international travelling experiences. He'd been to Bali twice and to New Zealand once. Each time had involved questions and X-ray machines. He began to doubt the wisdom of trying to get on the plane with diamonds stuffed in every pocket. So, just before the door of no return, he patted his top pocket, as though searching for cigarettes and turned around and went out of the terminal.

He got his Telstra van from the parking lot and drove to one of the service gates around the side. He beeped his horn until a security guy came. He didn't get out of the van. The guard waved and yelled. Dave waved his hand impatiently. The guard finally opened the gate. And Dave drove past him.

Dave parked his van near the baggage handlers shed and wandered in, yelling at the first guy he saw, 'You got a problem with the phones?' It was a safe question. Everyone had problems with their phones. But the guy shook his head and raised his hands and indicated a hearing impairment or too little English and pointed back to an office.

Dave nodded and waved, but as soon as the worker turned, he joined a luggage trolley heading out towards a Qantas jumbo connected to the departure gate number printed on his boarding pass. 'Is this the plane to Amsterdam?' he yelled.

'Man, you can't come out here,' yelled the baggage driver.

Dave pointed to the emblem on his shirt. 'Telstra.'

The guy was already driving away towards the open stomach of the plane. The engines were warming, whining painfully.

Dave went under the back of the plane near the wheels and up the rear steps where they were loading sealed containers of food and drink.

A hostess blocked his way, just inside the rear door. 'Hey.'

'Telstra.' He tapped his chest insignia as though it was a police badge. 'Your inboard communication system has problems?'

'You'd have to see the captain,' she said, pointing forward.

Dave stepped past her into an aisle where early passengers were getting seated. Another hostess stepped out, her smile on hard.

The first one said, 'Doesn't it get fixed by engineers?'

Dave reached into his envelope and produced his boarding pass and waved it at both of them. When they looked confused, he said to the hostess who'd met him, 'Just professional interest.' Then he turned to the hostess in the aisle and said, 'I wandered back here for a look. I'll come back later, when you're not so busy.'

Dave wandered down the aisle, with his boarding pass out and a studied expression of seat-searching, fighting the tide of passengers coming the other way.

He found his window seat but someone was in the way. In the aisle seat sat the beautiful woman who had smiled at him from the airport newsagents. Serendipity is a glorious thing when the converging items aren't jeeps and Telstra vans. He put his empty carry-on in the overhead locker, then gave the woman his winningest smile. 'I can hoist myself over, or we can shuffle?'

She stood and stepped out into the aisle and Dave slid and sat too heavily on one of the mounds of rocks in his back pockets. He gasped.

The beautiful woman moved back into her seat with a swish of knees from her ruffling skirt, looking at him oddly.

Dave said, 'So, flying eh?'

'Yes. That's what my ticket suggests.' She reached for a magazine.

Dave considered this first rebuff as no more than part of the process like, say, the haka before a good rugby game. He offered his hand, smiling. 'Angus MacFergus.' He thought that next time he said it he might try to put a bit more Scots spittle in 'Fer'.

She said, 'And don't tell me. You work for Telstra.'

Dave looked down at his shirt in shock. 'How did you guess?'

Dave saw her supress a smile. There was hope. She had dark brown eyes and dark hair and a kind of perfect Italian nose.

'And you are?'

'Not looking to make a new friend.' She opened her magazine and started reading. She hadn't said it that rudely. It wasn't irrevocable.

Dave adjusted a couple of the rock bulges in his back pockets. 'I'm betting that by around the thirteen hour mark, I'll have worn you down.'

'Given that this flight goes to Singapore and that's only five and a half hours, those will be very long odds.'

'My favourite kind.'

Her name was Margaret St James and he did wear her down but somehow she got ahead coming off the plane from Singapore to the Netherlands and Dave couldn't seem to push through all the other passengers to catch up to her as they filed into Schiphol airport. Then he saw the two dodgy business guys up ahead. They were scanning the passengers. The younger one was tall and tanned and fit-looking. The older one was in his mid-fifties, with an angry red face and rumpled body. They stood with a new thin man in a much better suit. The thin man talked into a walkie-talkie, also examining the incoming passengers. Dave finally felt the prod of alarm and ducked away to the toilets.

He went into a toilet stall and considered a new plan. Every pocket of his pants was stuffed with the uncut diamonds, the delivery of which would bring him twenty thousand somethings, which it was not unreasonable to assume was cash. Twenty thousand was a very good number to be dealing with, given the debt to Mungo. It was seriously worth the punt.

Dave figured he might as well get comfortable. He emptied

the stones from his pocket into the carry-on bag and joined the dazed and addled line of passengers trudging to customs. He had his passport ready. He felt his breathing go shallow, his pulse begin to get up towards the happy level. He recalled that in many airports today, apart from having men in dark uniforms carrying machine guns, there were also cameras pointing at the incoming. Trained professionals, possibly mothers and priests, scanned the faces of passengers looking for signs of guilt. Dave wondered if the mounting excitement he felt as he approached his customs official would be mistaken for guilt and unleash the machine guns.

'Hello,' said Dave to the customs man as he handed him his passport.

'Good morning, sir,' he said. 'Anything to declare?' Before Dave had time to manufacture his lie, or make up a really good joke, the customs man looked over Dave's shoulder.

Dave turned. The thin man in the good suit stood examining Dave, his left hand cupping his chin, his index finger tapping on his pursed lips. He looked past Dave, and nodded, precisely.

'Thank you sir,' said the customs man. 'Have a nice stay in the Netherlands.' He put Dave's passport on the counter and looked up for the next passenger.

A more circumspect man, given to cosmic questioning, might have taken a moment at this point. Dave, on the other hand, believed in gift horses and never looking them in the mouth. He picked up his passport and walked through.

Dave stood in the freezing wind looking down at the houseboat. It was sagging and badly in need of paint and possibly a bilge pump. It was dark inside.

Dave looked back at the row of well-preserved three-storey brick buildings squeezed along Amstel, Centrum. They had shiny brass number plaques and warm yellowish glows from upstairs windows. Across the canal were other houseboats and street lamps and pretty trees. Dave barely had time to note its olde-worlde charm before a cruising police car sent him scurrying onto the deck of T.0.59.

He hurried to the door of the upper cabin, pushing it open to reveal wooden steps leading below. 'Hello. Um, Angus, here,' Dave called.

He moved slowly down the steps searching the wall for a light switch. There was one at the bottom of the steps, but it clicked uselessly. Dave bumped into a table and then a chair before he found a curtained window. He pulled the curtains open, allowing in some dim yellow light from across the canal. The cabin was threadbare and dusty. There was a kitchenette and a dining room table with a kerosene lamp. He put his bag of diamonds on the table and got a thin blanket from the bunk bed built under the stairs.

Dave went to a door at the end. 'Hello. Angus MacThingie here.' He opened the door to a little toilet and shower. He went back to the bag of diamonds and put it under the pillow of the bed. He sat on the bench seat under the window shivering in his thin Telstra shirt. He was cold and hungry and tired. He could use a beer. He looked at the bag poking out from under the pillow under the stairs. He got the bag and emptied the stones into the drawer in the kitchenette. He stood, shivering, and looked out the window. Across the canal, on the wall of a big building, the sign said Amstel Diamonds. 'The glamorous world of international diamond smuggling,' said Dave, a little ungraciously.

There were many bridges and many women sitting in windows in their underwear. There were blonde women and dark women, fat women, gaunt women, African women, Thai women, Japanese women. There were women who may not have been women.

Men window-shopped, occasionally being let in the front door.

Dave roamed, freezing and hungry. He passed 'video cabins' with X-rated signs in neon pink, Live Shows, Live Girls, sexual memorabilia shops, marijuana cafes amidst the Heineken signs. And there seemed to be drunken youths from every country in the world stumbling and staggering with forced laughter amidst the red and occasionally green lights.

However, Dave could not find a real shop. He needed warm clothes. He asked some young guys who replied in American accents. 'You can get sex and drugs twenty-four seven, but try buying toothpaste.' 'Or a decent hamburger.' 'All the shops shut at six.'

A man in a black leather jacket stopped next to them to light a cigarette.

Before Dave could approach him a Moroccan youth appeared in front of him. 'Hey, how you going? Havin' a nice time?'

Dave doubted he was the diamond contact, but said, 'I'm Angus MacFergus and I'm cold.'

'Cool. Cool man,' said the Moroccan. 'You want anything? I got ecstasy. Really good gear.'

'How much for your jacket?

The Moroccan wore a denim jacket with a fleecy collar. 'Jacket? What's that? I can get anything, man. Not sure we call it that here.'

'Your jacket. I'll buy your jacket. And some warm pants.'

'Fuck you, man. You want that, then go to the flower district. I'm selling drugs.'

The offended youth pointed his finger at Dave then lost tension and floated away with the other pedestrians. The guy in the black leather jacket was talking to his cigarette packet but caught Dave watching and turned away before Dave could make an offer on his jacket.

Dave saw a bright blue and red parka ahead. It was on a young guy outside a shop window where fat African women were gyrating in their underwear to no discernible common rhythm. The parka looked waterproof. It looked like it was full of some eiderdown or equally Nordically-tested warm material.

Dave tapped the youth on the shoulder. 'How much for your jacket, mate?'

He said, 'Fifty euros for the fuck and suck,' in a French accent.

'How about fifty pounds?' Dave peeled off a fifty from his envelope.

The youth in the parka stepped back and abused Dave in seemingly unpunctuated French. The youth's two mates slapped the French youth on the back and pushed him in the chest, laughing and obviously urging him to accept Dave's unintended offer.

'The girls, not me,' the youth finally said in English.

Dave raised his arms in apology. 'Sorry, mate. I want to buy your jacket. I'm freezing.' Dave took out a hundred pounds and waved them.

One of the African prostitutes banged on the window and gestured for them to move off.

'Why should *I* freeze?' said the French guy.

'Two hundred pounds.'

More French. His friends were urging him on. 'Get his shirt. It's cool,' said one of them pointing to the Telstra shirt.

'Okay,' said Dave, 'jacket, pants and shirt. Two hundred pounds for the lot.'

Dave looked around for a place to change then dug another fifty-pound note out of his magic envelope and waved it towards the African prostitutes behind the window. The door opened and Dave and the French guy and his mates all piled in. The African ladies started yelling in Dutch. The French guys started assuring in French. The African women smiled and started speaking French to the boys.

There was now no room to change in the window area so Dave grabbed the parka youth by the elbow and started up the stairs.

A big Maori stepped out on the landing above. 'What's going on down here?'

'Just a bit of a fashion parade, mate. Hands across the ditch?'

'Not bloody likely.' The Maori looked past Dave and yelled, 'Hey, what are you lot all doing in here and not buying?'

'They're making sure this man doesn't try things,' said the Frenchman.

'How about ten pounds for the use of the room? To change. Mate, I need some warm clothes. You can chaperone. Two minutes.'

'Chaperone, yes,' nodded the French guy.

'Twenty,' said the Maori.

'The All Blacks are losing it.'

'Thirty.'

'Fair call.'

The Maori opened a door to a tiny, windowless room. There was a single bed, washstand and tiny dresser. The ceiling globe cast a smoky blue light.

'Very classy,' Dave said to the Maori bouncer as he went in.

'I'll thump you,' offered the Maori, mildly.

Dave took out thirty pounds and gave it to the Maori, and then another two hundred pounds and handed it to the young guy. He peeled off his Telstra shirt and his pants. The French kid was doing the same but watching Dave very warily.

As they swapped clothes Dave became aware of a slightly different tenor to the general commotion downstairs. He could hear a loud Aussie voice. 'Let's go darlin'. I like 'em big and meaty, like me. Up this way? Fifty euros eh? Only place in the world where the prices haven't gone up. You know, I reckon I've been in here before. Hope they've changed the sheets.' The

Aussie swayed into the doorway. It was the older businessman from Perth, from Schiphol. He was puffing from the stairs, his face bright red and sweaty.

'You,' said Dave in alarm.

'Oh, sorry. Room's full huh?' He winked at Dave then fixed his eyes on the French kid now dressed in Dave's Telstra shirt.

One of the African prostitutes had pushed up onto the landing outside the room, and the Australian bumped into her as he turned away. 'Changed my mind.'

'Hey,' said the Maori looking from Dave to the other Australian. 'What's going on?'

The Aussie pulled a mobile phone from his pocket and said, 'Contact. Go, go, go.'

The Maori slammed him to the wall. The African prostitute screamed, her bright red bra and the landing wobbling dangerously.

Dave grabbed the red and blue parka and started out of the tiny room, squeezing upstairs through the threesome of large people on the landing.

The front door was being pounded. The French guys and the other African prostitutes howled and pushed back against the door. 'Descente de police!'

Dave clambered up another flight of stairs, turning to see the Maori and the Aussie grappling on the landing. The French youth ran down the stairs. The front door gave way and uniformed policemen pushed through the screaming Africans and yelling French. They rugby-tackled the Telstra shirt. Then the Australian and the Maori fell, tumbling down onto all of them amidst the screams and yells of a pretty good scrum pack.

Dave raced around the bend and found an open window. There was a fire escape and he slithered down it into a series of alleys filled with garbage and the smell of urine and the sound of many scurrying things, smaller than Dave.

Dave came out further up the street. The flashing blue mixed prettily with the red lights coming from the brothel window and the yellow from the street lamps. It was the light. It was frozen in balls in the night like ... like ...

Dave nearly crashed into Margaret, who was berating a man in staccato Dutch. She turned to see Dave in surprise. 'Angus!'

'You speak Dutch,' Dave said.

'I shouldn't come along here at night,' she said, indicating the departing man. 'Nice jacket.'

'I'm trying to blend in, like a native.'

'I'm never going to get rid of you, am I?'

'Can't fight good luck.'

She raised an eyebrow, but then took in the commotion down the street. 'Actually, if you wouldn't mind, you can escort me out of here. I'm getting sick of the attention.'

'Okay. Can we eat?'

They went away from the police action, Margaret switching into tour guide mode. She'd explained on the plane that as part of her travel agency she regularly saw the sights so she could tell her clients first-hand where to go. She'd already told Dave where to go a few times by that stage. As they walked Margaret pointed out historic areas, listed the seafaring history of the Dutch and explained why the cyclists might be getting angry with him—because he kept blundering across the dedicated cycle lanes.

And then they were back by another canal and standing in the middle of a high stone bridge looking at the yellow lights flickering in the dark water. She pointed across the canal. 'There's a wonderful restaurant up there next to Amstel Diamonds.'

The sign looked familiar. Dave looked to the other side of the canal. 'You're not going to believe this, but I live up that way.'

'You're kidding! You don't. In one of those gorgeous houses?'

'A little closer to the waterline.'

'What does that mean?'

'I'm in a houseboat.'

'How wonderful. That's not a bad idea for tours. You know. Fly to Amsterdam and stay on a canal.'

'Well, I don't think they'd be keen to stay on mine. More your hovel boat.'

'Oh? Why are you staying there?'

'Ah, that's a long story.

'You seem to be good at those.' She stood smiling at him, some lamplights gleaming from her eyes.

'Enough about me. Let's talk about you and me.'

'Is this hovel boat one of your compulsions?'

'Huh?'

'On the plane. You said you were the impulsive type. Compulsive impulsive I think you said.'

'And you remembered. Told you I'd wear you down.'

'I think it was somewhere after Singapore. Not that you wore me down. But I must have been listening at some point.'

'Ah, good, I think.' There was a small boat coming along the canal with its lights on. Dave looked towards the Amstel Diamonds sign and where he supposed food was cooking. Margaret didn't seem in any hurry to leave the bridge.

He said, 'I was listening to everything you said. I believe you told me you were married.'

'Yes?'

'But there's no ring.'

'Maybe I'm simply not wearing it.'

'And maybe you were lying.'

'Why would I do that?' She smiled. She was enjoying herself.

'Maybe you thought it would put me off.'

'Whereas it made no difference whatsoever.'

'Maybe.'

'You are right. I am a liar.' She was flirting and she was good at it. 'Are you?'

'What?'

She studied him a moment, then looked towards the Diamonds sign. 'It looks too busy.' There were some Volvos and a dark van all manoeuvring for parking spots nearby.

She suddenly squeezed Dave's arm and said, 'Let's go to your houseboat.'

Dave could not quite believe his luck. He managed to gasp, 'Yes.'

She took back her hand and looked down, a little shy, but then she looked up and said, 'See, I can be impulsive too.'

Dave leant to kiss her, but she stepped past and he missed.

He lit the lamp and turned it down. Margaret stood examining the inside of the houseboat.

'So you reckon it might not make your tour list, huh?'

'It did look better before you lit the lamp. Authentic would be the real estate word.' She went to the window and looked out on the water. 'Must be a policeman's birthday.'

Dave went to the window and looked out. 'What do you mean?'

'At the restaurant.' She looked at him.

'What?'

'The police Volvos. The vans with tinted windows.'

Dave looked across the water. 'Are they?'

She drew the curtains and they both straightened together and she kissed him. It was gentle and she tasted like white wine, but as he tried to kiss her more fully she stepped back, crinkling her nose.

'Hold that thought, lover. I believe you smell.'

'Testosterone?'

'Possibly. Or twenty hours on a plane with a hint of three different kinds of very cheap Middle Eastern perfume.'

'Ah. I stink huh?'

She nodded, still smiling. 'Nothing a shower and shave and clean teeth and nakedness won't fix.'

Dave's mind went blank, like he'd put everything on the last race and was waiting for the start.

She was speaking again. 'What say I meet you in there?' She pointed to the bunk under the stairs.

'You bet.'

Dave had shaved and showered as she'd instructed and stepped out of the bathroom and into the main room of the houseboat in Amsterdam wearing nothing but his best smile. Margaret was waiting for him.

Unfortunately, also waiting were two men.

'Oh,' said Dave on seeing the men in the dim kerosene lamplight. They looked as displeased as Dave felt.

'Angus,' said the tough-looking one in a thick Scottish accent. He stood blocking the stairs leading up to the deck.

'Ah,' said Dave.

The Indian man held a briefcase and looked from Dave to Margaret. 'What the ...' he said in a London accent.

Margaret got up from the table. 'Angus, you've obviously got things to do. How about we take a raincheck. I can see this isn't a good time.'

'Wait,' said the Scot. He had scars crisscrossing both cheeks. 'Whit's she daein' here?'

'I just met her,' said Dave.

The Scot looked from the bunk bed to Margaret to Dave and then down to Dave's shrunken aspiration. 'Ye just met her?' He didn't look like he believed any of it.

'On the plane,' said Dave.

'And the brothel?' asked the Indian.

'Getting a jacket. It was cold. Speaking of which.' Dave gestured towards the pile of clothes by the bathroom door.

'Well, whatever was going to happen won't now,' said Margaret with what Dave was sure was regret. A lot of regret. 'If you'll excuse me gentlemen?' She took a step to get past the Scotsman, but he grabbed her handbag.

'Hey,' said Dave.

'Ah doon't like surprises. Let's see who we've ... Ah. Deary, deary me.' He pulled a plastic bag full of uncut diamonds out of Margaret's handbag.

Dave stood blinking, hurt.

'Sorry, Angus. They looked valuable, and well, I did tell you I was a liar. I suppose I'm also a thief. Nothing personal.' She fluttered her eyelashes.

'Evidently not,' said Dave, feeling further diminished.

'Whit ye goot gooin' here, Angus?' asked the Scot. 'A doublecross?' He looked over to the Indian, then to Dave again.

'Why would I travel all this way before I did it, if that's what I was going to do?'

The Scottish heavy passed the plastic bag of stones to the Indian, who had his briefcase open on the table.

'Gentlemen,' said Margaret, edging towards the stairs. 'You've said nothing yet that in any way implicates anyone. So, I know nothing and I'd rather not know anything.'

'It's no' up to ye to "rather" anything.' He was continuing to block her.

Dave said, magnanimously under the circumstances, 'Come on. No harm, no foul. You've got the stones.'

'We'll see aboot that.' He looked towards the table. 'Karushi?'

The Indian whose name was evidently Karushi, had an eyeglass to his eye, examining the stones. He scratched one with a metal prod.

Dave thought he heard a thump outside. Maybe dripping water. Margaret seemed to have heard it too.

The Scot was watching Karushi. 'Well?'

'Mostly shit,' he said in his thick London accent. He flicked a smaller rock away. It shimmered. 'This one's gem quality. The rest are industrial. And no pinks as requested.'

Dave nodded knowingly.

'Speak fookin' English.'

'Geologically, these are them. A lot of fuckin' fuss for not too much. But it's what the Gov ordered.' He shrugged, good soldier.

Another thump. Then a loud voice outside. It was a woman, yelling in Dutch.

The Scotsman looked up.

In spite of her rather tight skirt, Margaret launched a sudden but seemingly precise kick, karate style, into his knee.

He fell to the floor, groaning. She picked up her handbag and stepped smoothly up over him onto the steps. He grabbed her ankle before she could go further, but Dave launched himself across the room onto his shoulder. Margaret scampered up the steps.

Dave heard her say, 'I owe you one, Angus.' He didn't have time to reply, because something hit him on the head.

Dave woke but didn't open his eyes. He could hear a familiar Scottish voice. 'Och, naw, Mr Dewar. He was as surprised as anyone. No' t'first lad to be ripped aff by his dick.' Dave could feel the slight movement of water under the barge. He was shivering.

A voice talked through a phone like the echo of an angry bee. Dave opened one eye. He was on a mobile. 'Ye wahnt ah tae dae 'im and bring t'stones?'

Dave tried to see if there was anything he might use as a weapon.

'Oh aye.' He clicked off.

Karushi said, 'So, you doing him, Campbell?'

The Scotsman, who now finally had the name of Campbell,

said, 'We're tae bring 'im tae Glasgow. Have ye got t'condoms?'

Dave sat up. 'Whoa there. Now I know this is Amsterdam, but ...'

'Doon't flatter yirself, Angus. Get dressed. What did ye think ye were goonae dae wi' that wee thing?'

'It's cold.'

As Dave got dressed, Karushi funnelled batches of the tiny stones into each condom.

'Hope ye've an appetite,' said Campbell pulling a bottle of scotch from the briefcase. He filled a tumbler and pushed it across the table towards Dave.

'Good news, Angus,' said Karushi. 'We thought we'd have to do this.'

Dave took a gulp of the whisky. 'So how much money, again?'

'Twenty thousand.'

Dave eyed the growing pile of condoms.

'And we won't kill you.'

Dave stood uneasily near the departure gate in Schiphol. His legs were rubbery, partly from all the whisky he'd drunk, but also from the strange sensations the lumps in his stomach were causing.

Karushi pushed a cheap backpack under his arm. 'The hotel address is in the bag.'

Campbell patted him on the shoulder. 'Ye wait there until we come. Naw wee love affairs.'

Dave nodded. He was pushed towards the departure gate. He walked very carefully.

He sat very still on the plane. He didn't try to make new friends.

He asked the taxi driver in Edinburgh to go round corners as slowly as he could.

He stood against the wall of the charmless white and magenta room of the Jurys Inn trying to work with rather than against the movements inside his body. There was a faint smell of vinegar somewhere in the room. The condoms of rough diamonds continued their slow progress like obese worms heading south. The whisky had worn off.

The battered telephone shrilled centimetres from his ear.

The vigorous Australian voice at the other end said, 'Ken, it's Bruce. A quick call while you're alone. Mal's still in hospital in the Netherlands, but he'll be here soon. Okay?'

'Okay,' said Dave.

'I'm still with you, mate.'

'Mate.'

'Here they come.' Bruce rang off.

Dave had no idea who Bruce was or why he had called or who Mal was, but he'd sounded Australian and that was comforting so many kilometres from home.

The hotel room door opened and the Glaswegian Campbell and London-Indian Karushi walked in to find Dave holding the phone.

'For fook's sake, whit's going on noo?'

'Room service. I ... more whisky?'

Campbell studied him, but Dave closed his eyes, still standing.

'Naw, ye already have a full toommy. It's time to retrieve oor packages.'

'I've got a bit of bad news about that. I'm not ready.'

There was a pause. Dave heard the telephone dialling.

'We're here, but we have a wee hold-up. The stupid bastard's constipated.'

Dave could hear the other side of the conversation. Another Scottish voice. 'Noo matter. T'woman in Holland bothers me. Bring him tae Perth. Ah'll meet ye at Scone Castle.'

'Scone Castle!' exclaimed Campbell.

'Aye. I want ye tae take t'train up. Look tae see if ye're being followed. There's something no' right here.'

Karushi fed Dave Indian takeaway on the train up to Perth. There were lots of lentils. 'To get things moving, like.'

An ancient castle crouched atop an outcrop above Stirling. It had clung there for centuries, a piece of historic tenacity that Dave found alarming. Each bump and roll of the train brought aftertastes of the Indian food. Dave sweated. Dave winced. Dave tried not to think about anything, especially when the train entered tunnels.

On another day Dave might have been quite interested to discover that there was another place called Perth in the world. He might have relished the ancient stone wall the taxi drove through and the ivy-covered battlements and lush grounds of Scone Castle. But today he had more immediate concerns. There were tourist buses in the car park and a line of old people winding towards four portable loos not quite hidden behind a screen of bushes. They were frail people easily pushed aside by a driven younger man.

'I gotta go,' said Dave.

'No' yet,' said Campbell.

They led Dave, who walked with a stoop, towards a small church on a small hill in front of the castle.

A ruddy man in his mid-fifties sat on a worn sandstone block. 'Angus, or should ah say Ken,' he said in the thick Scottish accent Dave had heard on random telephones across the globe. The man stood and raised his arms to encompass all that they could see. 'Welcome tae centre of Scotland, laddie. Home tae oor true government for at least thirteen hundred years.'

'Uh, huh.'

'Ah'm James Dewar and this hill is Boot Hill because t'lords of every kingdom would regularly arrive here and empty their boots of dirt. Dirt from their own dear lands tae swear fealty tae their king. And over centuries they made this hill.'

'Yup,' said Dave, when Dewar paused.

'And noo ye've brought a little of yir own land here, and ah need ye tae empty yir boots, so tae speak.'

'Gladly.' Dave looked hopefully towards the tourist line at the toilets down the hill.

'This stone is a copy.' Dewar was pointing to the sandstone block he'd been sitting on. 'T'Stone of Scone is where oor kings were made, but fookin' Edward ripped it off. Held it, and Scotland, tae ransom in fookin' Westminster Abbey.'

'Ah, about emptying my, ah, boots.'

'Oi. Ah huvnae finished. Ye see t'Scots heard Edward was a coomin', so ye think they let him get t'real stone?' Dewar tapped the side of his nose and grinned like an insane person. 'It's somewhere, but no' in Westminster and no' in Edinburgh.' He tapped his nose again, leering at Dave. 'T'Scottish huv nivver given up on oor fight wi' England.'

'Good for you.'

Dewar looked at Dave with clear disappointment. He looked at Campbell and Karushi and then back at Dave. 'Ah wis led tae believe Australians are noo friend tae English.'

'Um, well, you know. I think we got a lot of it out of our system when we made *Breaker Morant* and started winning at the cricket.'

Dewar looked confused.

Dave said, 'I'm more a mercenary than a revolutionary. Sorry.'

Dewar threw his hands up in disgust. 'Aye.' He said to Karushi, 'Over t'graveyard.'

Dave turned and started trotting down the hill, like a hobbled prisoner, towards where Dewar had pointed. On consideration, he'd take the graveyard, even if it meant death. Two young hikers who had been taking photographs of the chapel scrambled back away from them. One looked vaguely familiar.

Karushi caught up with Dave and directed him under an arch and around into the old much-breached wall of the cemetery.

He handed Dave a plastic shopping bag and pointed to some particularly high moss-covered headstones.

'You're kidding.'

'Hurry up before the tourists come.'

'No peeking.'

Karushi turned away.

Dave got behind the largest headstone and took down his pants and felt a surge of relief. But then the relief was replaced by pain, the pain of attempting to squeeze particularly large, non-viscous … … camels through the eye of his needle.

Dave and Karushi headed back, Karushi holding the plastic bag out in front of him, as far as his arm would allow.

Dewar and Campbell met them on the path near the entrance to the castle. When Karushi handed over the bag Dewar exclaimed, 'Ye could huv washed it.'

'Where?' Karushi wiped his hands on the stone block.

Dave, who felt bruised and abused but otherwise better, said, 'Well, I've done my bit. More stones for Scotland and all that. Go the revolution. Now will that be cheque or cash?'

Dewar looked around in alarm. 'No' here, man. Go wi' t'lads. There's a hire car in t'car park.'

'What, I can poop here, but not get paid?'

'Go wi' Campbell, Ken.' Dewar turned away, holding the bag out to his side, downwind from his nose.

Dave was pushed to a tiny jellybean of a hire car, a bright blue Ford Ka. Campbell looked at the key and then the car with disgust. 'In t' back, Angus.'

'Look, I'm sure you fellas need to get on with things. So, here's fine. It doesn't have to be exactly twenty thousand pounds. A tip for your trouble is only fair.'

'Shut up,' said Campbell pulling back his jacket to reveal the gun Dave had always suspected he had.

'How about this? You keep everything. And I'll chalk it up to experience. With gratitude. I'm an older and wiser man.'

'Get in the back.'

Dave got into the jellybean blue Ka, and thought quickly of many things, none of which would save his life, but all of which he would try.

(From *Now Showing*, short fiction, 2013.)

# ROBERT EDESON

# THE WEAVER FISH

Within the opaquely threaded dialects of the Ferendes, and in all the languages of all the coasts that share their latitude, there must be ten thousand distinct words for weaver fish. More words than reported sightings. More words than actual fish by now, possibly. And more words than the number of fishermen who have use of them.

The latter is logically, if speculatively, explained by Thomas MacAkerman's observation that each person uniquely owns a private, talismanic name, as well as sharing the communal vocabulary, itself vast. Since MacAkerman's time, the accumulated effort of a distinguished rollcall of anthropologists, sociologists, and linguists has generated no more plausible a theory.

More surprisingly, modern oceanography and marine biology, for all their sophistication, seem to have advanced our knowledge of the fish itself not at all. Except, of course, to amplify its mystique and elusiveness. No specimen having been caught and dissected, there is yet no scientific nomenclature, no genus, no species. *Acarcerata textor* might serve, when the need arises.

MacAkerman was a physician and amateur naturalist, of catholic interests and impressive breadth of scholarship, who accompanied Captain Joseph on HMS *King of Kent* for two voyages, in 1816 and 1819. An enthusiast of the new sciences, he was apparently a brilliant popularist and quite famous for his public lectures. These, unfortunately, were never edited for publication, though their quality can be inferred from the comments of contemporary diarists. He did author several papers and monographs on varied subjects, but in respect of the weaver fish only two primary sources survive. One is a short entry, bearing his initials, in the first (and only) edition of the *New Scottish Encyclopaedia*. The second is a letter in the *Transactions of the Philosophical Society of Edinburgh*, of April 1823. MacAkerman there describes how, shortly after sunrise on Greater Ferende, he was exploring the littoral for crab species when he 'occasioned' on a large sea-pool, sequestered from the receding tide by a sandbar, and

> about a half-fathom in depth at its most. My attention being focused in pursuit of the crustaceans, their size and colour and actions, I did not at first see something altogether more interesting, which I took then to be some optical phenomenon of the sand and water. I walked the circumference of the pool, to see it vary in place and intensity, and with light in front and behind. It took many minutes to discern, and then only in half belief, that I was seeing fish swimming, many hundreds of them, and of the most transparent substance imaginable, except for small eyes, themselves faint, so that what I had witnessed was the movement of eyes, and a changing refraction of the pool sand of great subtleness. My interest in crabs for the moment set aside, I watched for perhaps a half hour, then something impelled me to throw dry bread into the centre, expecting I don't know what, but I hoped for some intensification of visible movement. What did follow I

could not have expected, for I could not wildly invent the sight, nor would I wish to, for it recurs to me in most distressing images and waking dreams these last seven years. The bread floated for some moments in several pieces, without noticeable disturbance, nor any interest of the fish. Then a solitary gull, to whose aerial squawks I had been only half attuned, plunged at the feast, and rather than plucking one bit in flight, settled on the water, intending, I fancy, to enjoy the multiplicity. Then followed an event I would wish on no man's conscience, and I am sorely in need to expunge from mine. In an instant the water rose in symmetry around the gull, but it was not water, but a mass of fish stacked high, as well as I could see from the disposition of their eyes and the faintness of their bodies, in intercrossing alignments of great discipline that was surely not accidental. The wretched bird attempted flight, but to nought avail, as its legs seemed bound in a viscous gel. Then the fish trap (I should call it) rose higher to the full measure of its hapless victim, which soon became lifeless, appearing I thought as encased in ice fully a half foot above the water surface. The orchestration of the trap was now more evident, fish bodies tightly woven crisscross, like warp and weft, but layered, as a solid tapestry might be made, and quite still. And before my eyes, the gull dissolved. I repeat, the beast dissolved in minutes to skeleton alone, but for a strange purple colouration (which I would name Tyrian) surrounding it. Then abruptly, as if on some regimental bugle call, the whole edifice unweaved, the pool returning to its former state but for the gull bone sinking unimpeded at its centre, not five yards from where I stood.

> I confess then to great perturbation in my heart. Where previously I had thought lightly of entering the water for the better inspection, I was now repelled, I should say fearful, and stepped back from its edge. For if they could rise so deliberately above its surface, could they not breach its boundary also? After some minutes of composure, and my anxieties abated, I resolved to learn more, and taking from my wares a fine pole net I set about straining the shallows from a discreet distance. To my delight I soon scooped one, a half yard in length as they had all appeared, and held it up for transport to the sand. But to my astonishment and sore disappointment this triumph was quickly reversed. For the fish, which made no movement throughout, took on the purple hue that I had noted earlier, though more intensely, seeming to secrete or gurgitate a slime that I can only guess was some digestive acid of the greatest potency, for almost in a second the fabric of my net was burnt and through its deficiency so effected my captive escaped, falling to the water where it was instantly invisible. Standing there, with my net made useless for its purpose, I admit to the strangest feeling of defeat and perplexity, which in all my years of collecting God's creatures has no equal before or since.

MacAkerman goes on to describe further unsuccessful attempts to ensnare a specimen, but his efforts were eventually frustrated by the returning tide. It is difficult now to judge how this account was received. It was a time of a growing culture of wonder at the natural world, with a proliferation of gentleman scholarship that was rarely challenged. The last vigorous debate was on infinitesimals, and the next would be evolution. The modern critical discourse of science was in its infancy. Thus there was no subsequent correspondence on the topic in the *Transactions* or any other journal. None of this, of course, should be taken to impugn the accuracy of MacAkerman's report. He was, from all the evidence, a man of unimpeachable integrity and intellectual rigour whose contribution to the sciences has few parallels in his era. Only many years later, and then only in the practice of medicine, was his judgement disordered by the cruel and tormenting decline of his final illness.

There is no doubt that MacAkerman's discovery had a profound influence on him. In a public lecture series of 1824 (abstracted by the canal engineer James Lypton in his *Journal* of that year), he explained his motivation for the second voyage in 1819 as 'to further my researches in the natural history of the weaver fish' (the exact wording may be Lypton's). As it turned out, he never did acquire the specimen for which the Old World museums would have bid dearly; indeed he reported no further observations with any confidence.

But that is not to say the voyage was a failure, and at least two major achievements can be ascribed to 1819. First, he completed the collection that would form the basis of his definitive work on tidal crab speciation (long before Darwin's ideas were published), and secondly, he conducted what we would now call field ethnography among indigenous fishing communities, centred on language and folklore pertaining to the weaver fish. The latter is a fragmented opus surviving only in notebooks, journals, and many secondary sources, and greatly deserves the attention of modern scholarship. From these studies, we learn that the majority of names for the weaver fish have roots in native words for death, water (that is, a fish made of water), invisibility, the colour purple and, of course, a woven cloth or matting. These meanings were so concordant with MacAkerman's own observation that he was persuaded that similar sightings must not have been infrequent, though obtaining witness testimony proved more problematic. In any event, MacAkerman first employed the term 'weaver' in 1816, apparently quite independently of any native tradition, and never varied from its use. Paradoxically then, whilst no synonyms exist in English, he has left us with a monumental foreign lexicology far exceeding that of any other single referent.

In 1916, exactly one hundred years after MacAkerman's seminal observation, a fisherman named Josef Ta'Salmoud, from the village of Madregalo on Greater Ferende, saw weaver fish. Ta'Salmoud himself gave only a brief description of his experience, and was never persuaded to repeat or enlarge upon it. But there are many eyewitness accounts, from villagers on the shore, which are fully corroborative of what he described. Some of those present were still alive in 1996, and were interviewed by this author during a Language Diversity Initiative field trip. It should be said in this regard that more research is needed using newer validation tools applied to both linguistic and thematic elements. Authentication studies also require a good understanding of cultural specifics in oral tradition, which can be very localized and idiosyncratic. This work is continuing as part of a wider LDI programme.

On days following severe night storms the fishing grounds of the Ferendes could be deceptively treacherous. It was customary for the chieftain of fishermen to enter the water first and, having ascertained conditions in the bay, signal to those on shore that they should remain there or join him. One morning, Ta'Salmoud set forth on this task. As was normal, his progress was observed closely by those on the beach. When he was about fifty yards from shore he stopped paddling and stood in his canoe, facing the villagers. To this point, nothing seemed unusual, and they next expected his signal. None came.

> The bay was rough with a big sea swell and a bad current. I stood in my canoe to give the signal: do not come out, I am returning. I thought, be careful, Ta'Salmoud, stand safely, these are the times—rough days making the signal—when my ancestors have drowned. But when I got up, suddenly the bay was calm and my canoe became still. I could have stood on one foot. I thought, I have been wrong, the bay is smooth. Then I saw water in my canoe, with little holes in the hide, and purple colour near my feet. When I saw the purple I knew it was the kenijo before I saw the kenijo themselves. The water came up to my canoe side, but it was the kenijo weaving, but water from the sea was inside, on my feet. I was thinking, I must give the signal to save my fisherman brothers, but I don't know if I did. I was so full of fear. Then my canoe was full of water, but not sinking because I think the kenijo kept it there. For as far as I could see there was the weaving, like a thick mat on the top of the sea, and I thought, Ta'Salmoud, you must run for your life and even though I thought I would die I stepped from the canoe onto the weaving fish mat and it seemed very strong. My feet sank only a little and my good balance from standing in my little boat kept me from falling. I took another step, and another, then I started to run. I knew that if I stumbled I would be eaten but I kept running. Every place that my feet touched there was a purple mark, and my feet hurt but I hardly looked down. I was looking at my village and my people. They said later that I was crying out my word all this time but I don't remember that. To me it is like a terrible dream, until I see my feet.

From the village beach, these events must have appeared truly astonishing.

> It was very strange. When Ta'Salmoud stood up the rough water became smooth. Not like wind stopping but as if it was made into glass, all in a second. I thought, what signal will he give? Then his canoe sank and he just stepped onto the water and ran to us. The whole village was quiet. Poor Ta'Salmoud, he was saying over and over his word, not shouting, but very softly but we could all hear it. We all knew it was the fish. I did not breathe until he was safe, and then I did not breathe when I saw his feet. I don't know when I breathed again.

Not even the sight of a man running on the surface of the sea prepared the villagers for what they next saw.

> When Ta'Salmoud was close to the shore he stopped running, I think as he felt the sand under his feet. He was still saying the word, and we could see his face was very frightened. He came from the water and was bending over like an old man. We were too frightened to go to him, and all of us stayed quiet. I could not look away from his feet but I could not look at them also. Then Maria [Ta'Salmoud's wife] stepped forward and took his hands, but she was looking downwards too. I think Ta'Salmoud then stopped the word and started crying, and I thought his face is not fear but pain. But we still stayed back, and Maria held him closer. He seemed in much pain and then he looked down, at his feet. From his ankles down there was no flesh, just bones and sinew, all purple stained. Poor Ta'Salmoud cried out and fell to the sand, in Maria's arms. He was half man, half rinlin. Purple rinlin.

The last word translates (somewhat inadequately) as skeleton, which is surely exaggerated. Presumably, the digestive secretions of the weaver fish had destroyed the skin and much of the soft tissues of his feet. There is no doubt that the foot bones below the ankle joint were exposed, but we must suppose that sufficient blood supply and other attachments were preserved to maintain rudimentary function. Sensory innervation was clearly compromised, for he was not in constant agony as we would otherwise expect. Only when his feet became dry did he suffer pain, and this was quickly assuaged by immersion in seawater. Almost certainly, the cleansing action of the latter practice minimized the bacterial contamination that in these circumstances would ordinarily lead to suppuration, fasciitis and fatal septicaemia.

It is said that as Ta'Salmoud collapsed on the beach, the calm in the bay vanished, replaced in a moment by the most frightening storm the villagers had seen. For Ta'Salmoud, then, the weaver fish was not an agent of disfigurement and pain, but of salvation, providing safe deliverance from the temper of the sea.

Not surprisingly, the news of a fisherman who apparently calmed the sea, walked upon water, and suffered uncomplaining an unspeakable injury attracted the attention of the Church. In 1921, papal envoys visited the Ferendes to investigate the claims and determine a recommendation of sainthood. They declared in the negative on the grounds that, though the events truly occurred, they were not miraculous but explained by natural causes, namely the weaver fish.

There is one known photograph of Ta'Salmoud, taken during that visit, and protected under *lex Vaticani* (it may be viewed but not reproduced). He is at the centre of a small group, standing on the beach with the village behind. The others are bowed, but Ta'Salmoud's head is high, looking not at the camera but into the distance beyond. Almost certainly, he is staring at the sea. The photographer was clearly not a scientist, for what we would like to have had recorded is an image of Ta'Salmoud's feet. But the manners of the time, or ineptitude of the nuncio, have forever denied us this evidence. While his companions' feet are all on view, Ta'Salmoud's are hidden by the tub in which he stands, presumably immersed in his anodyne seawater.

Ta'Salmoud died, from all accounts peacefully, in the following year, 1922. He had never fished again, nor ventured into the bay. All the stories attest to him being treated with the greatest reverence, and after his death his word, *kenijo*, became the main word, the most precious word, and the most protective one, for all his descendants. There is something poignant about a great fisherman who had walked on the sea, thereafter to be made forever to stand in it, in pots and pans and ignominious tubs, or at the water's edge, half in half out. Half man, half *rinlin*.

(From *The Weaver Fish*, a novel, 2013.)

## K.A. BEDFORD

# AUNT JULIA GOES UNDER

*Pelican River, 192–. The widowed Ruth Black brings Aunt Julia home from the hospital to convalesce in the sleepy fishing town of Pelican River. Ruth enlists her friend Gordon Duncombe to help her get to the bottom of Aunt Julia's nightmarish encounters with the Other Side.*

Rutherford brought the great vehicle to a stop out front of my home. He climbed down and came around to help Julia and me disembark. Doing this, he settled into the usual routine, ordering the three other staff about, getting young Ryan to come and help with the luggage, and asking Sally Hall if she and Vicky Tool had made up a room for Miss Templesmith, as per his telephoned instructions. Sally said they had prepared the Yellow Room, next to mine, thinking that Ma'am would want her relative close by. I greeted everyone, and told them they were doing a fine job, as always. Though I did pause as Ryan went by, and said, 'The new hair cream not working out?' He coloured and said, 'No, Ma'am, sorry, Ma'am,' and struggled into the house, bearing more luggage than his skinny body looked capable of carrying. I introduced Julia to everyone, and in particular to Sally and Vicky, and instructed them to take the very best care of her. 'Aunt Julia's not been well, and is in need of a good pampering.' They agreed and escorted her into the house.

Julia, however, was staring around her at the house—a modest red-brick two-storey Federation-style property with an extensive verandah all the way around. One of the house's most novel features was the circular windows here and there, like portholes on a ship. 'It's bigger than I thought,' she said, smiling weakly back at me. She was also staring at the enormous, but very strange-looking, paperbark gums looming around us, their pale, peeling trunks looking as though they had some terrible skin disease. Native birds cawed and squealed and carolled noisily; the breeze carried the salty tang of the sea, and a faint waft from the fish canning factories on the foreshore. Julia, swatting at flies, seemed all at once aware, as she looked at these alien trees and heard those unusual birds, that she was indeed somewhere very different, and very far, from home. I knew she was an inveterate traveller, but she had never come this far, as if to another world.

Rutherford looked at me, concerned, and I could see he was wondering if bringing Julia here was a wise decision. I, too, was having second thoughts about this, but resolved to adhere to my plans. I told him to take the car around to the garage and give it a clean; it was white with gravel dust. 'Yes, ma'am, as you say.'

In the quiet coolness of the house, with its high ceilings, polished jarrah floors, tasteful but unfashionably minimal furniture, I breathed in the complex aroma of home. I could never describe its exact scent. Part of it was the very air of this region of Western Australia, part was the native-plant pot pourri, part was the fresh smell of a house kept meticulously clean, part was the lingering traces of last night's fire in the big fireplace. There were many elements, and I treasured them all. No house in England would ever smell like this. I remembered the grand, stuffy, echoing manorial homes in the old country, much like my own family's house, with its thirty-two rooms, all of them cramped with too much heavy furniture, maddeningly busy wallpaper, ancient heirloom floor rugs, hunting trophies, sombre portraits of long-dead ancestors looking like they hated the artist and the fuss of having to get all dressed up when they'd much rather be out with the hounds and the horses and all their inbred chums. By contrast, I had determined this house I bought would be full of air and light; it would never be stuffy; it would be welcoming, not intimidating; and comfortable without that cloying cramped feeling I still remembered and hated from my old life.

I joined Julia in the Yellow Room, where she was having a word with Vicky. Before entering, I heard Julia ask, 'What on Earth would make a sensible girl stay in such a place, I ask you!'

I interrupted, knocking pointedly on the door. 'Now now, Julia, you mustn't harass my staff like that. Is everything under control, Vicky?'

'Yes, ma'am,' she said, not stuttering too much today. I sent her to help Sally.

'Well,' Julia said, sitting on the bed as if worried it might eat her. 'You appear to have created a very nice little realm in the midst of all this chaos.'

'Chaos? What do you mean?' I knew very well what she meant.

'Do those birds ever shut up? And what's all this ...' She lacked a word for it but simply waved a hand at the view through the window, which showed extensive natural bushland: gum trees, wattles, grevilleas; it was marvellous, and I had gone to great trouble to preserve as much of it as I could. I had never, when I first arrived, seen such native bushland. It was exotic, alien in every respect. I could not stop looking at it, marvelling at how such unusual plants could possibly survive in such an arid environment. The people who sold me this house had offered to get people in to clear all this 'clutter', to make it, 'you know, suitable'—whatever that meant. The only concession I had agreed to was the stipulation that I allow a clear area around the garden's perimeter. I found out about this from the land agent when arranging the purchase of the house. He told me the perimeter was in case of bush fire, and I stupidly asked what exactly that might entail. 'It's the end of the world, Mrs Black,' he explained. Feeling foolish, I agreed, and allowed a clear perimeter. Trying to get a lawn to grow on the cleared land, however, was another matter.

I explained to Julia about the bush, that it was something fundamental to the landscape in this country. Julia glanced at me as if to suggest that I was the one with problems in my head. 'But it's just so awful! It's so wild and uncontrolled!'

Later, Julia and I sat in the drawing room. She kept looking around the great room. 'How do you manage with all this ... all this *space* everywhere?'

After lunch, I rode my purple Imperial Racer bicycle around to Gordon Duncombe's house. Gordon lived on a small farm on the outskirts of town; he had converted the great barn, its old wood long turned greyish-silver, into a workshop-laboratory. Even before I arrived, his dogs—twelve of them—erupted into a deafening barking frenzy. As I opened the front gate, and wheeled the bicycle inside, the dogs, mutts all, swarmed around me, jumping, barking, wagging their assorted tails. Expecting this, I had brought a small bag of meaty offcuts which I doled out with great care. None of the dogs lunged or made as if to bite me. They accepted the idea that they would have to wait before receiving their treats. Once it was all handed out, the dogs wagged off, going about their own business on the extensive property, and I walked my bicycle up the long gravel drive to the house.

Gordon, who would have heard the dogs, stood waiting on the front porch, under the verandah. He was in his fifties, a soft sort of man with a slight stoop, as if having trouble bearing the weight of the world.

He smiled. 'Ruth! What a grand surprise—and here, I've just put the kettle on, too. Coffee?'

I thanked him, and he took my bicycle, as usual, and walked it up under his verandah, where it would be safe in case it rained. I followed him inside, careful the dogs didn't bowl me over as they boiled around my legs. I knew they each had names, but I had not yet learned them, even though I heard him talking to these dogs all the time. They kept him busy. He, for his part, kept his house surprisingly tidy and clean. The odour of dog was rarely detected in his modest house, despite the menagerie.

In his cozy lounge room, I took a seat on the old couch and Gordon sat across from me in his favourite overstuffed brown chair, with its very large rounded arms. No sooner had he sat than two of his dogs appeared and leapt straight into his lap. He yelled, shooing them off, 'Come on, you lot, get out of here! We've got company! Yes, that's right. There's someone else in the world apart from you mongrels!' The two dogs stared for a moment, then trotted off, tails high. He looked at me, a little embarrassed. 'Sorry about that. What a madhouse!'

I rather liked that it was such a madhouse, to be honest, but I didn't want to tell him that, in case it sounded somehow patronising or condescending. I liked that things were always happening here, that there was such a lot of life about. I loved my own home, for its peacefulness, for its grounds and for its view of the distant Estuary, but it was a house for quiet contemplation and reflection. Gordon's house, by contrast, was a place for making things happen.

I explained the situation with Julia.

Gordon's manner changed, growing serious and thoughtful. His lounge room, as with much of the small house, was full of jammed bookcases, none of which matched, just like his dogs.

The whole collection looked like something put together over time by someone with limited funds but a great passion for books and knowledge. As rickety as the bent and straining shelves looked, I knew he had some wonderful old books, and not all of them were science and engineering texts. He was soon up on his feet and perusing his shelves, squinting hard because he was too proud to get spectacles, and then he would complain about fierce headaches. This was something we argued about a lot. I knew he would much rather buy a book than something as useful and practical as spectacles. He would rather buy a book than clothes. Most of the time he would rather buy a book than food, too, if it came to that. He managed on sandwiches and crackers and soup, and was generally hardly even aware of food. It was a tedious necessity. I had only seen him sit down and enjoy a good meal for its own sake when I invited him to my home for a friendly dinner; he always had to have a notebook with him, or a technical journal, or a new book open on his lap or next to his plate. And his plates often went cold if inspiration should strike mid-meal. Gordon and I talked a great deal about creative impulses and what they meant, how they worked. Such conversations inevitably boiled down to Gordon ruminating about the functions of the human brain and how it must work in order to produce the kinds of things it could produce.

He came back into the room, bearing a thick book. 'You say Julia seemed to speak in a different voice, almost, describing things she had never seen, but describing them correctly ...'

'Yes. And, of course, killing me.'

'Hmm, yes ...' Already he was off again, skimming lines of minute text. 'How do you feel about hypnosis?'

Surprised, I stared at him. 'Pardon?'

'Do you think she'd agree to going under?' He sat in his old chair again, book open in his lap.

'She might ...' I really had no way of knowing. I did know she was deeply worried about what might be going on in her head, though I had not discussed with her my darkest, most alarming fears: that something had taken root in her brain, in a place where it would not appear to her consciousness. 'I suppose it couldn't hurt,' I said.

I invited Gordon to join us for dinner that evening.

He laid out the evening meal for his dogs before we left. As usual, he purchased the finest cuts of beef he could afford for them, meat that would grace a table for nobility, while no doubt contemplating a strawberry jam sandwich for himself and perhaps a fortifying cup of sweet tea. It is strange when one finds oneself envying the food of dogs.

I telephoned for Rutherford to come and fetch us, and at length, we left. Rutherford did the honours with my bicycle, gently placing it in the Bentley's immaculate boot, where it looked small in the great space. He greeted Gordon, too, with genuine respect, 'Good afternoon, Mr Duncombe. I trust you are well today?'

Gordon, who came from a decidedly working class background in the English Midlands, had a difficult time dealing with the idea of servants. It never occurred to him simply to speak to them as he would to me, for example—and he had had enough trouble working out how to address me, too, in the beginning, because of the ridiculous class nonsense. He regarded them as some sort of posh automaton, to which one must speak extremely carefully for fear of the thing going on a crazed rampage of destruction. He'd been attempting to deal with this for some years now, and had, lately, decided to try a strategy of simply nodding and repeating back the main greeting. He said, 'Afternoon, Rutherford,' and looked relieved to have achieved this much. He climbed into the back of the Bentley, still marvelling at the space and appointments of the car, and sat a respectful distance from me. I suspected he would love to talk to Rutherford about the engineering aspects of the car, but I knew that he never would, because who knew what the Rutherford-thing might do in retaliation?

Back home, I informed Murray that there would be another guest for dinner. I knew already that Gordon would not stay the night even if our discussions ran late. He needed to look after his dogs, who fretted, he said, if he was away from home too long. Murray nodded, said, 'Right you are, ma'am,' and went back to the kitchen, ready to terrorise poor Ryan, her apprentice, afresh.

I took Gordon inside. Rutherford asked if Sir would care for a drink, and Rutherford asked for a cup of tea, three teaspoons of sugar, thank you. The same as always. Rutherford disappeared to prepare the drinks. Whilst we waited, I fetched Julia, who had been napping. Waking, seeing me, she smiled. 'I say, what a perfectly splendid bed!'

Ah, something that met her approval, at last, I thought. 'Will you be joining us for dinner, Julia?'

She perked up further. 'What's on the menu tonight? Your cook would not say.'

I smiled. 'Murray is like that, I'm afraid. I don't know, either. Dinner is always a surprise. Murray takes these things very seriously. Dinner must be an event.'

Julia looked nonplussed. 'But you know how my stomach is, Ruth. There are –'

I knew, of course. One could not help but know about Julia's 'delicate' internals. I explained that I had already taken the liberty of briefing Murray on Miss Templesmith's dietary concerns. 'All will be well, fear not.'

She looked happy for the first time since I had seen her. I thought this would be an opportune moment, and mentioned that I had invited my old friend Gordon Duncombe to dinner as well. Julia liked meeting new people—after all there might be a fortnight's stay at their estates on offer at some point—and brightened considerably. Julia, at least in the old days when I knew her, spent much of the year staying at a succession of friends' and relatives' estates; she was hardly ever actually home. I explained that Mr Duncombe was out in the drawing room as we spoke, and that he might have some useful thoughts about her condition.

'Is he a medical man?' she asked, climbing out of bed and searching for decent clothing—which Vicky had left folded on the chair.

'Mr Duncombe is something of a Renaissance man, if you will.'

'I see,' she said, washing her face and hands. 'Known him long, have you?'

'We met shortly after I settled here. And no, we're not "like that". Gordon is a very good friend. He's also an inventor of things, I might add, and he dabbles a little in magic.'

She looked at me in the mirror. 'Magic? Rabbits out of the hat stuff, then?'

'Not as such. I mean he dabbles a little in what one might call "real" magic. As well as his inventions.'

'Extraordinary,' she said. 'These days, I gather, most true magicians work for the government or conduct research at universities.'

I was surprised to hear this. I had never known.

'So your Mr Duncombe. He builds things, and dabbles in the other as well? How remarkable! Can he fly?'

I smiled. 'Not with magic, no. He is attempting to build a time machine, though.'

'I say. He could scarcely be more colourful, could he?' she said, amused.

A few minutes later, I had made the introductions. Rutherford hovered nearby offering to fetch things as required. I asked him what time dinner would be tonight. 'I believe dinner service will commence at half past six. And no, I do not know what Murray has planned. Discreet study of her shopping lists and ingredients would suggest, perhaps, a roast, but this could merely be one of her ruses.'

Gordon was talking to Aunt Julia. 'Ruth has told me a great deal about you, Miss Templesmith, if you'll pardon my saying so.'

Julia looked amused. 'Pardon me for asking, but is that a West Yorkshire accent, Mr Duncombe?'

'Fourth generation, born and bred, as they say. Whereabouts in England are you from, if I might ask?'

I rolled my eyes. Gordon had just opened the Box of Doom. Julia started in, probably unable to believe her luck. 'Well, and this is a fascinating question, one on which I have spent quite a considerable sum these many years, though I must first preface my remarks by saying that the Templesmith country seat —'

I interrupted. 'How's your tea, Gordon? Need a refill?' I glared at Julia, who smirked.

He glanced across at me like a man suddenly aware he is in deep waters without a life preserver. 'Yes, please. Thank you.' Rutherford provided the fresh cup almost as soon as Gordon had placed the request.

Aunt Julia wisely adjusted her approach. 'Ruth tells me you are building a *time machine*, Mr Duncombe?'

He looked up from his tea, face slightly flushed. 'Ah, well. Yes, or rather, trying to, at any rate,' he said. 'There have been some technical, and possibly conceptual problems, at least so far —'

'Tell Julia how you destroyed your own barn—twice!' I said, teasing gently. Gordon did his best not to be flustered.

'It was the wrong voltage, and in any case, I had no way to know the capacitors were full, now, did I?'

Julia was quite taken by the thought of travelling through time. 'I've read Mr Wells' marvellous book, many times. It's one of my favourites. I do admire those hard-working Morlocks, don't you, Mr Duncombe?'

Gordon, looking pleased to find a like-minded soul at last, leaned forward in his seat. 'Speaking strictly confidentially, I can let you know that I am in occasional contact with Mr Wells, through the post. He *assures* me that the book is a carefully disguised memoir.'

'You are pulling my leg!' she said, amused, watching him over her teacup.

'I should think not, Miss Templesmith,' he said, a little nettled.

It was time to intercede. 'Julia, I believe Gordon might be able to help with your condition, somewhat.'

She looked up, blinking, surprised, at me. 'Oh yes. Yes, of course. Mr Duncombe, you are also a medical man?'

Gordon looked concerned, frowning a little, and he took a long draught of his tea. 'I have been something of a dilettante in my reading over time, but I could not claim to have studied medicine formally.'

'My niece informs me that you are also versed in the ...' She looked like she felt awkward about using the term. 'In the magical arts. That you "dabble", as Ruth put it. Is that quite safe?'

He ran a hand through his thinning hair. 'Oh, well, yes, ah, yes. Absolutely. You take all the right precautions, and do everything according to standardised procedures. It's no more dangerous than working in any of the physical sciences, I should say.'

I interrupted again. 'My Aunt Julia, Gordon, is neglecting to mention her own abilities beyond what one might call the strictly empirical. Isn't that right, Julia?'

She quickly smoothed over any appearance that she was miffed to have her sport spoiled, and said to Gordon, 'Since I was a girl, I have been able to see other parts of reality, Mr Duncombe. Parts not readily apparent to *other* people.'

'Indeed?' he said. 'What do you see?'

Julia, surprised out of her wits, stopped and stared at him. All her life she had been accustomed to either lack of interest or outright scepticism or condescending comments of 'Of course you do, dear ...' No-one in her life had simply asked her, straight out, what she could see. At length, I saw she looked very different. She looked, for her, vulnerable. When she spoke, her voice lacked its usual brisk humorous tone. 'Well,' she said. 'I see all sorts of things. I ...'

Since she had been surprised into speechlessness, I prompted her. 'Tell Gordon about your dreams.'

'Ah, yes, yes of course,' she said, looking at me with relief. To Gordon she explained about how, shortly before she embarked on her epic journey out to Australia, she had begun having dreams 'qualitatively different' from the colourful dreams that were her normal experience. And when Gordon gently prompted her to describe these dreams, he saw, as I had in the hospital, the change stealing over her. She sat differently. Her voice dropped into a flat, deep—and very sad—monotone. Her eyes stared at things only visible from inside her mind. Gordon listened, transfixed, to the narrative as the voice described entering my house without difficulty, without alerting either Rutherford or Young Ryan, and then the business-like search through my post, my modest collection of heirlooms, and then into my study upstairs where the voice described a thorough, professional investigation of my desk's contents without any interest in the stack of manuscript pages piled next to my faithful Imperial typewriter. At last, the intruder made his way, without hesitation or searching, to my bedroom, where he negotiated the door without effort, and then ...

I interrupted, shaking Julia's shoulder vigorously. She seemed to wake as if from a deep sleep and glanced about at our horrified faces. 'Oh dear,' she said, upset, 'it happened again, didn't it?'

'How is your head feeling now?' Gordon asked, without any of his usual politeness.

She touched her head delicately. 'It's rather sore, I must say. I feel somewhat ... weak, I'm dreadfully sorry. Perhaps I should go and lie down.'

I did my best to reassure her that all was well, despite her insistence that things were clearly not. I asked Rutherford to fetch a stiff drink for her, and she did not, unusually for her, protest.

'Gordon, any thoughts?' I asked.

After Rutherford retreated, Gordon looked concerned, but also confused. 'There are many worrying aspects, I must say. The ability of whoever it is to move through the house—and it's clearly this house, no question—without making a sound is most troubling. Particularly since the outer doors are locked, as a matter of course ...'

Julia was surprised. 'You lock your doors?' Back home, village life was still such that locks were rarely needed. Here, things were different.

I said, 'Julia, listen to him. He has an idea.'

Gordon explained his notion of hypnosis. This wasn't a form of any kind of magic. Indeed, he had only learned about it after reading Sigmund Freud's texts on psychoanalysis; Freud employed the technique extensively in order to access areas of the mind not readily available to one's conscious perception. It was a controversial technique. The medical establishment, most particularly the neurologists, argued that Freud was a fraud, and that he was making up his findings as he went along, and quite possibly harming as many patients as he claimed to help. Nonetheless, the technique of hypnosis had been with us for many years. Julia had heard of it, but only in the carnival sideshow realm of things.

'Are you sure it's quite safe?' she asked Gordon. He said he believed so, if one went about it with the right precautions and minimised the time in which the hypnotic subject was 'under'.

'I must confess,' he went on. 'I do not have a great deal of practical experience with it. But I think, if we –'

'Ruth, dear. What do you think?' Julia asked me.

'I think it might help. But it is of course up to you.'

'Will you be quite gentle, Mr Duncombe?' she said, and allowed herself the tiniest of mischievous smiles.

Gordon, noticing, blushed. He gathered himself. 'I will do my very best for you, Miss Templesmith.'

'Then let's have a try,' she said.

Dinner that night was a grand construction featuring roast duck at its centre. Another triumph for Murray. Julia, who put aside her anxiety about her dreams long enough to enjoy seconds, sat after each of four courses, exclaiming, 'I could not possibly eat another bite!' while Gordon, another healthy eater if someone else was going to all the trouble, leaned back and complained, 'It's that after-Christmas-dinner feeling all over again!' As Ryan and Vicky cleared away the clutter, I excused myself from the long table and nipped back to the hot and aromatic kitchen where I congratulated an exhausted, damp-faced Murray on another excellent meal. For her part, she only nodded, and pointed out how it could have been so much better, and 'bloody Rutherford' had not helped by spying on her in order to find out what was on the menu. 'You'll need to have a word with him, ma'am. If you don't, I will!' She was serious. She was always like this. No wonderful effort was ever good enough for her. She always apologised for various parts of the creation. It was like God apologising for cloudless sunsets.

Much later, Gordon, Julia and I sat in the drawing room, close to the fire, enjoying a brandy. Gordon took forever over his brandy, as always. He was not accustomed to such things. He wanted to make it last as long as possible, without looking impolite about it. Julia, by contrast, finished hers quickly and asked Rutherford for another. He lifted an eyebrow, but I allowed it. Julia, full of dinner and wine, was talkative, perhaps more even than usual. She was telling Gordon about her childhood in the draughty, crumbling Braethorn House, where she could escape from nannies and governesses and even her mother for hours at a time, exploring secret passages and huge, long-abandoned rooms where the furniture was draped with dusty sheets and you could still hear, when the weather was right, the ancient house settling into its foundations, even after so many centuries. She told Gordon about her encounters with ghosts ('Most of them terribly sad people,') and fey wraiths of no discernible character ('Creatures of pure feeling, one might say,') and, once, an outlaw thief hiding in an abandoned wine cellar ('He stayed three weeks, and I brought him food, but I had to be so careful, Mother and Father suspected something was not right and their kitchen staff were reporting that food was going missing ...')

'Did you get caught?' Gordon asked, intrigued.

She smiled. 'Yes, of course. I was only a silly girl. I was no match for a house full of suspicious relatives and servants.'

'What happened?'

'As it happened, they packed me off to a boarding school for nine years.'

'That seems harsh.'

'The outlaw I was helping had, apparently, also murdered a family of four. He hadn't told me that part.'

'Careless of him,' I said.

Boarding school, for Julia, was a miserable experience. She hated the regimentation, the constant press of other students, the lack of privacy, the punishing study routines, the pecking order. Indeed, she ran away three times, but was always caught. And one time she almost set fire to her dormitory, but a nervous confederate confided to the staff before it could happen. The one thing Julia had liked about Ashling School for Girls was that it, like the old family estate, was teeming with ghosts. She got on well with them, since the great majority of ghosts were deceased schoolgirls who had come to bad ends, some by their own hand. Julia understood how this might happen in such a hideous place.

The old clock on the mantel was chiming midnight.

Gordon looked up. 'Is it that late?'

I nodded, politely swallowing a yawn. Julia said, 'Oh dear, I've been prattling along for hours! Ruth, dear, you should have told me to put a sock in it long ago.'

'I did try,' I said, smiling.

'Mr Duncombe,' she said, 'exactly when shall we conduct this hypnosis business? Right now would seem an opportune moment. There's nothing like midnight, if you ask me, for venturing into the hidden realms of things?' She smiled at him, her eyes alive in the firelight.

'Gordon?' I looked at him, wondering how he felt. He would be thinking about his dogs.

He swirled the remains of his brandy. 'I suppose it couldn't hurt, could it? Shouldn't take long.'

Julia beamed, excited. 'Right, then! What do I need to do? Am I all right sitting just here, or should I move to a more conducive chair?'

He told her she was just fine where she was. He fished out his sterling silver pocketwatch, given to him by his own family when he reached his majority, more than thirty years ago. The case was elegantly engraved; it would fetch a sizeable sum at auction, should he ever be foolish or desperate enough to sell it. 'All I need you to do, Miss Templesmith, is to relax, take deep, slow breaths, and keep your eyes on my watch here.' He sat on a stool before her, and dangled the watch from its fob chain; it turned this way and that, glittering like liquid gold with reflected firelight. 'I want you to relax as much as you can, from the tips of your toes, all the way up to the top of your head. If you feel a need to settle back in the chair, please feel free. I just want you to relax, relax, perhaps think about some of those favourite places from your childhood, and keep watching the light on the watch here ...'

I had to force myself to look away; I was feeling rather sleepy myself. Soon she had drifted away into a state somewhere between awareness and sleep, and she curled up in the large chair, looking like nothing so much as a little girl. She wore a small smile. The firelight flicked across her face.

'Now what?' I whispered, trying not to sound too impressed.

'First, we give her a subconscious trigger so that we can bring her back to consciousness immediately if anything worrying occurs. Then another trigger that can be used, in the future, should we need to induce this state again.'

'Why would we want to do it again?'

'It's what Freud does, though there I suppose he's thinking about recurring weekly visits.'

We decided to omit the latter trigger. Soon Julia was ready.

Gordon took her back to her home, more than three months earlier, to before she began experiencing the disturbing dreams. At the time Julia had been living at the country home of her cousin Jeremy, an earl, and his wife, Countess Mary. It was a modest holding, four hundred acres, in a picturesque valley not far from Leeds. 'What do you do each day, Miss Templesmith?'

She spoke in a quiet, sleepy sort of voice, and described wonderful meals, extensive reading of newspapers and novels, visits into Leeds for afternoon tea with local friends, visits to the library each day for fresh books, evening walks through the hills with Jeremy and his dogs. It sounded like a wonderful, uncomplicated sort of life—except for the manner in which

Julia was handed around between all the relatives. She did not like her own home these days, but could not bring herself to sell it and move; this was the family estate: it had to remain in the Templesmith family, even though she was the last of the direct line.

'All right,' Gordon said, 'let's go to the first night you experienced the dream.'

Julia looked anxious, shifting in the chair.

Gordon said, 'It will be all right. Nothing can hurt you.'

She settled. He proceeded.

Julia went on to describe the first dream, which, perhaps disappointingly, consisted of no particular distinct imagery, but instead a growing sense of cold unease that built, slowly, into panic—and then something indefinable that made Julia blurt out my name, gasping, as if afraid for her own life.

'Bring her out, Gordon!'

Julia was greatly distressed, crying now, *'Oh my God, Ruth! No, not Ruth!'* She went on and on. I gathered this was how it had been, that first night. Gordon interrupted, and brought her away from the source of that fear, brought her back to a safe, quiet place. She calmed. I dabbed at her tears with my handkerchief.

'Now what?' I said.

'We need to find out where this is coming from. It seems unlikely that, in the middle of an otherwise serene sort of life, she should suddenly get upset over something to do with her niece, whom she hasn't seen in years. Makes no sense.'

'I would not say we are close, but we have always gotten on well, after a fashion.'

Gordon went back to Julia, and asked her if she could go back to the point where she first felt that anxiety. She nodded, and said, fidgeting already, 'All right. I can feel it. It's cold. I'm so cold.'

'Where is the cold coming from, Miss Templesmith? Is it like a wind or a breeze?'

She looked confused for a moment, then 'looked' to her left. 'Yes ... yes, I can feel it coming from ...'

I was feeling cold, too, listening to this, and wondering where Gordon was going.

'Julia, I want to see if you can move into the wind. Can you do that? Can you see where the cold wind is coming from?'

She was shivering, but looked determined. It was easy to imagine the child Julia looking like this on finding a secret passage in the old house, and intent on finding out where it went, regardless of the possible danger of exploring in a darkness lit only by candle or lamplight. 'I can feel it growing stronger. It's ... so cold ...' I could see her chin trembling a little. She rubbed at her arms. I fetched a blanket, and Gordon used suggestion to help her feel more protected from the wind.

'Tell me what you see now, Julia?'

'I'm ... I'm in a sort of tunnel, or a passageway. It's very dark. The floor creaks. Things are fluttering around my face. Moths, I think, perhaps. There's a bad smell. I'm not sure. I can just barely see.'

'How is the wind?'

'Stronger. Much stronger. It's ...' She frowned. 'It's hard to press ahead.'

'You have the strength to get there, Julia. You have the strength.'

'I'm not sure I want to get there. I'm scared. It's ... not just cold. There's something else. Something bad.'

'Gordon? Is this wise?'

He glanced at me. 'I'm not sure how many chances we'll have to do this.'

'Be careful!'

He nodded. 'Julia?'

'Yes?' It was a little girl's voice.

'Can you go on?'

'I want to.'

'Let me know if you want to stop. Just raise a finger or use the trigger word, all right?' The trigger word was, prosaically enough, 'Exit!'

'All right.'

'What can you see now?'

'There's a light.'

'What sort of light?'

'C-candles, I think. There's a room.'

'Is the wind coming from this room?'

She nodded slowly, and looked very frightened. Her eyes still closed, she looked around. Whispering, she said, 'It looks like a cellar. Smells dusty, and there's old bottles and casks in racks, and some steps.'

'Is anybody there with you?'

She shook her head. 'No. There's just ... there's ... a circle thing ... on the floor ...'

'A circle on the floor?' I did not like the sound of this. 'Is it painted or drawn in chalk?'

'It looks like paint,' she whispered in the tiniest voice, 'but it doesn't smell like paint.' She wrinkled her nose. 'It's dreadfully bad ...'

'Is this a room you have seen before?'

Julia shook her head again. 'I've seen rooms like it. It smells.'

'Can you move into the room?'

Feeling tense myself, I said to Julia, 'It's all right, Julia. You're safe.'

But she was shaking her head again. 'It's not safe! It's cold here, it's cold! I'm freezing to death, it's, it's ... like a blizzard, I want to go!'

'Gordon, bring her out!'

He wanted her to stay under a little bit longer, to learn more, but Julia's desperation was all-too-palpable. 'All right. Julia?'

Julia suddenly gasped in fright: 'Someone's coming! Footsteps!'

'*Julia—exit!*'

(From *Black Light*, a novel, forthcoming, 2015.)

# CONTRIBUTORS

**K.A. BEDFORD** is the author of such recent books as *Time Machines Repaired While-U-Wait* and *Paradox Resolution*. He lives with his wife Michelle and dog Freckle in the radiation-blasted wastelands north of the river in Perth, Australia. He is twice winner of the Aurealis Award for Best Australian Science Fiction Novel. Look him up on Twitter, @kabedford.

**ALAN CARTER** was born in Sunderland, UK—long long ago and far far away. He now lives in Fremantle with his wife Kath and son Liam. He works as a television documentary director. In his spare time he follows a black line up and down the Fremantle pool. This extract is taken from *Prime Cut* (Fremantle Press 2011), which won the Ned Kelly Award for Best First Fiction. Its sequel, *Getting Warmer*, was published in 2013. The third Cato Kwong novel will be published in 2015.

**MARTIN CHAMBERS** was born in Perth, the son of two journalists. He is married and has two adult daughters. He has worked as a biologist, a tour guide, a whitewater rafting guide, a lab assistant, a publican, a kayak designer, a ferry skipper and in mineral exploration. Between episodes of cycling, kayaking, sailing or travel, he writes. 'The Pit' is taken from his novel *How I Became the Mr Big of People Smuggling* (FP 2014), which was shortlisted for the T. A. G. Hungerford Award.

**AMANDA CURTIN** has published, to critical acclaim, novels *Elemental* (2013) and *The Sinkings* (2008) and short story collection *Inherited* (2011). She is also a book editor, the current fiction editor for *Westerly* and a presenter of workshops for writers. She has a PhD in Writing and is an Accredited Editor. Being a mildly phobic kind of person, she associates white knuckles with summer, heights, small planes, yoghurt and tofu.

**PETER DOCKER** was born in Narrogin, Western Australia, the son of a motor mechanic, and grew up on remote Lort River Station, Coomalbidgup. He studied writing at Curtin University, Perth, and acting at Victorian College of the Arts, Melbourne. Never much of a pugilist, Docker has had his nose broken three times, suffered fourteen broken ribs, and one cracked cheekbone. Docker was once ejected from Steve's Hotel in Nedlands for fighting in the nude. Having been locked up in four states, Docker feels that the East Perth lock-up is the most conducive for writing poetry. Whilst a member of the Army Reserve, he was charged and almost court-martialled for his overenthusiastic (and perhaps inappropriate) use of high explosives. 'Nana Was Right' is extracted from *Sweet One*, Peter's third novel, following *Someone Else's Country* (FP 2005) and *The Waterboys* (FP 2011).

When **JON DOUST** was in primary school he played it safe, but as he moved through high school he developed a taste for the occasional rush of fear and trepidation. As a consequence he lived a dangerous and exhausting life until he met his second wife, who almost tamed him, and forced him to sit quietly for long periods. He began to write. He has not stopped. His first novel, *Boy on a Wire* (FP 2009), was longlisted for the 2010 Miles Franklin and his second, *To the Highlands* (FP 2012), was shortlisted for the White Knuckle Ride of 1968. The books are part of a series, One Boy's Journey to Man, that charts Jack Muir's rocky path to manhood—and Australia's rocky passage to nationhood. Jon is currently at work on the third novel: *The One-Fingered Hitchhiker*.

**ROBERT EDESON** was born in Perth, Western Australia, and educated at Christ Church Grammar School, the University of Western Australia and the University of Cambridge. He has been a consultant anaesthetist and researcher, publishing in the neuroscience, biophysical and mathematical literatures. *The Weaver Fish* (FP 2013), Edeson's first work of fiction, won the T. A. G. Hungerford Award. It features, inter alia, renowned linguist Dr E. O. M. Tøssentern, who vanishes into thin air during a balloon expedition. The extract reproduced here is taken from an address entitled 'Thomas MacAkerman to Josef Ta'Salmoud: A Century of the Weaver Fish' delivered by Dr Tøssentern to the Lindenblüten Society in Nazarene College, Cambridge.

**RON ELLIOTT** is a scriptwriter, director and academic, and author of the novel *Spinner* (FP 2010). 'Double or Nothing' is an excerpt from a novella of the same name, and is taken from *Now Showing*, a collection of crime related fiction (FP 2013). Ron's directorial credits include a noir feature film, *Justice*, and episodes of ABC programs such as *Dancing Daze*, *Relative Merits* and *Studio 86*. He has written for *Home and Away*, *Minty*, *Wild Kat*, *Ship to Shore* and the AFI nominated telemovie *Southern Cross*. Ron is currently writing a thriller novel, *Burn Patterns*.

**GOLDIE GOLDBLOOM** is the West Australian author of *The Paperpark Shoe* (FP 2010), which won the USA AWP Novel Award, and the Novel of the Year from the Independent Publishers Association, as well as a collection of short stories,

*You Lose These* (FP 2011). Her story 'The Chevra' won Hunger Mountain's 2013 Non Fiction award. In 2014, she received both a National Endowment for the Arts Fellowship and a Brown Foundation Fellowship at Dora Maar House in France. Goldbloom teaches creative writing at Northwestern University and is a well-known speaker at international writing conferences. She is also an LGBT activist and the mother of eight children.

**ADAM MORRIS** is an Irish-born author and the lead singer-songwriter for the Murder Mouse Blues Band. He has won numerous international awards for his songwriting and performs regularly throughout the world with Murder Mouse as well as being a much sought after solo performer. He is currently undertaking PhD studies at the University of Western Australia. 'Reunion' is taken from Adam's first novel, *My Dog Gave Me the Clap* (FP 2011).

**DEBORAH ROBERTSON** was born in Bridgetown, Western Australia. Her first book, *Proudflesh* (FP 1998), won the Steele Rudd Award for the best Australian short story collection in its year of publication. Her first novel, *Careless*, won the 2006 Colin Roderick Award and the 2007 Nita B. Kibble Award, and was shortlisted for the Miles Franklin Award. A second novel, *Sweet Old World*, was published in 2012. Deborah lives in Melbourne.

**JULIENNE VAN LOON** is the author of *Road Story* and *Beneath the Bloodwood Tree*. She won the *The Australian*/Vogel's Literary Award for *Road Story*, which was also shortlisted for the Commonwealth Writers Prize Best First Book (Asia and Pacific) and for the WA Premier's Book Awards for Fiction.

Julienne teaches writing at Curtin University in Perth, Western Australia. Her shorter works have appeared in *The Monthly* and *Griffith Review*. 'He Lost Her Twice' is an extract from her third novel, *Harmless* (FP 2013).

**DAVE WARNER** is the author of nine novels, including the winner of the 1996 West Australian Premier's Award for Fiction, *City of Light*, and six other non-fiction titles. Dave Warner originally gained national recognition as a musician-songwriter. His nine albums include the gold album *Mug's Game* and in 1992 he was the inaugural inductee into the West Australian Rock'n'Roll Hall of Renown. Dave has written for feature film, stage, television, radio and newspapers and has published a successful series of children's novels. 'Jasper's Creek' is an extract from his forthcoming novel, *Waiting for the Cyclone* (FP 2015).

www.ingramcontent.com/pod-product-compliance
Lightning Source LLC
LaVergne TN
LVHW091141080826
845145LV00008B/2222

*9781925161250*